"How do you know I'm not interested?"

Sam asked, reaching out and tracing the neckline of Olivia's robe.

She lifted defiant eyes to his. "When you returned my unopened letters, your feelings were spelled out loud and clear, Sam. I realized then that you'd never really been interested in me."

The movement of his fingers stilled against her skin. "I didn't want a letter from you, Olivia. I wanted you. But that hardly mattered, did it? You didn't give a damn about me, or the fact that I wanted you to be my wife."

His bitter words tore at her heart. Spinning on her heel, she turned to leave. But he caught her arm.

"Is that the way you still deal with things, Olivia? By running away? But where will you run to this time?"

Dear Reader,

During this holiday season, as friends and loved ones gather for Thanksgiving, Silhouette Romance is celebrating all the joys of family and, of course, romance!

Each month in 1992, as part of our WRITTEN IN THE STARS series, we're proud to present a Silhouette Romance that focuses on the hero and his astrological sign. This month we're featuring sexy Scorpio Luke Manning. You may remember Luke as the jilted fiancé from Kasey Michaels's *Lion on the Prowl*. In *Prenuptial Agreement*, Luke finds true love . . . right in his own backyard.

We have an extra reason to celebrate this month—Stella Bagwell's HEARTLAND HOLIDAYS trilogy. In *Their First Thanksgiving*, Sam Gallagher meets his match when Olivia Westcott returns to the family's Arkansas farm. She'd turned down Sam's proposal once, but he wasn't about to let her go this time.

To round out the month we have warm, wonderful love stories from Anne Peters, Kate Bradley, Patti Standard–and another heart-stopping cowboy from Dorsey Kelley.

In the months to come, watch for Silhouette Romance novels by many more of your favorite authors, including Diana Palmer, Annette Broadrick, Elizabeth August and Marie Ferrarella.

The Silhouette authors and editors love to hear from readers, and we'd love to hear from *you*.

Happy reading from all of us at Silhouette!

Valerie Susan Hayward
Senior Editor

THEIR FIRST
THANKSGIVING
Stella Bagwell

Silhouette
ROMANCE™
Published by Silhouette Books New York
America's Publisher of Contemporary Romance

To my family, and all families,
who gather together to give thanks and love.

SILHOUETTE BOOKS
300 E. 42nd St., New York, N.Y. 10017

THEIR FIRST THANKSGIVING

ISBN: 0-373-08903-1

First Silhouette Books printing November 1992

Printed in the U.S.A.

STELLA BAGWELL

lives with her husband and teenage son in south-eastern Oklahoma, where she says the weather is extreme and the people friendly. When she isn't writing romances, she enjoys horse racing and touring the countryside on a motorcycle.

Stella is very proud to know that she can give joy to others through her books. And now, thanks to the Oklahoma Library for the Blind in Oklahoma City, she is able to reach an even bigger audience. The library has transcribed her novels onto cassette tapes so that blind people across the state can also enjoy them.

Dear Readers,

I'm from a large family and we make a celebration out of eating, especially on Thanksgiving! This is a recipe I make every year during the holidays.

Hope you enjoy!

Stella Bagwell

Candied Sweet Potatoes

3 to 3½ lbs sweet potatoes
1 stick butter or margarine
1½ cups light brown sugar (packed)
½ tsp cinnamon
1 tsp salt
½ cup maple-flavored syrup
½ cup water

Peel potatoes and slice lengthwise, making slices about ⅜ to ½ inch thick. Melt butter in large, heavy skillet. Add potato slices, lightly browning all on both sides.

Sprinkle sugar, cinnamon and salt over browned potato slices, then drizzle with syrup. Add water to the whole thing, then gently fold all ingredients together. Don't worry if some of the slices break, those will taste just as good! Cover skillet and simmer over low heat for twenty to thirty minutes, or until potatoes are tender and glaze is thick and syrupy.

Prologue

"You want me to come there? For Thanksgiving?"

Olivia Wescott gripped the phone with one hand and groped behind her for a chair to sink into. She'd never thought she'd see Sam Gallagher again. She'd promised herself she'd never have to see the man again. Now here was his mother inviting her to the Gallagher farm!

"I know it's short notice, Olivia. Were you planning on spending the holiday with your parents?"

A dry laugh rose up in Olivia's throat, forcing her to swallow before she answered Ella's question. "No. They're out of town." As usual, she thought. "But Ella—"

"Oh please, no buts," the older woman broke in. "Kathleen would be so surprised and happy to see you. It would mean so much to her to see her old friend again."

Olivia sighed, feeling mixed emotions. To be honest, she would love to see Kathleen again, too. Kathleen had been her closest and dearest friend since their college days together. But she was also Sam's sister. It was something Olivia couldn't allow herself to forget.

"How is Kathleen doing?"

Ella's worried sigh sounded over the line, conveying just how concerned she was about her daughter. "On the outside, okay. It's the inside that still worries me. She needs her spirits lifted, Olivia, and a visit from you is just the thing to do it."

How could Olivia possibly lift anyone's spirits when her own were at rock bottom? And to go back to the Gallagher farm—no, she couldn't face Sam again, even if it had been four years since she'd last seen him.

"Ella, I just don't—" She couldn't think. Her head was whirling, trying to come up with anything to put Ella off. True, Olivia had sent Ella a letter just before she'd left Africa, to tell the woman she'd be back in the States. In it she'd invited Ella to call her and give her an update about Kathleen. The last thing she'd expected was an invitation to spend Thanksgiving with the whole family!

"Olivia, I haven't told Kathleen or any of the family that you're back from your relief work in Africa. I wanted you to come home for the holiday and have it be a big surprise. Please say you'll come."

How could she possibly say no? How could she say, *I'd love to see Kathleen again, Ella, but I don't want to come to the farm and have to face Sam?* It just wasn't possible to tell her. Ella didn't know that Olivia had once loved her son. As far as that went, no one in the Gallagher family had known it. Except for Sam. And in the end, her feelings hadn't mattered to him at all.

The thought stiffened her spine and swept the doubts from her mind. She wasn't going to let Sam Gallagher keep her away from her friends! He'd hurt her in the past. She'd be damned before she'd allow him to hurt her now.

"Of course, I'll come, Ella. I'll be there as soon as I can get things ready."

Chapter One

The walk from the barn to the Gallagher farmhouse was a short one, but long enough for Sam Gallagher to hunch his shoulders against the frigid blast of wind and wish it was spring in Arkansas instead of late November.

On the screened-in back porch, Sam gave his boots a quick swipe on the mat, then looked pointedly at Jake and Leo, two collies that had followed him to the house. "Okay, boys, you either decide to stay on the porch tonight or go to the barn. Make up your minds."

As if they understood every word their master spoke, the two dogs hurried over to a corner of the porch and flopped down on a bed of throw rugs.

Sam entered the blessedly warm kitchen to find his mother, Ella, and his sister, Kathleen, standing at the gas range.

"Sam, come over here and taste this chili." Kathleen motioned him to her side. "I've told Mother it's too bland, but she won't believe me."

"Humph." Ella snorted while she continued to stir a pot of bubbling cranberry sauce. "I've already put in three jalapeños. Kathleen's just trying to see if she can make us all breathe fire tonight."

"We're having chili for supper? I wanted turkey and giblet gravy." After hanging his coat on a peg by the door, Sam crossed the room to join the two women. "Hi, sis, good to see you tonight," he said, bending his dark head and placing a kiss on his sister's cheek.

Kathleen reached up and gave his chin an affectionate tweak. "It's not Thanksgiving yet, dear brother. So you'll just have to wait for the turkey."

Kathleen quickly scooped up a spoonful of the chili, then held it out for Sam to sample.

He chewed, swallowed, then smacked his lips. "Good, but it does need another pepper, Mom."

The tall, dark-haired woman threw up her hands in surrender. "You kids are going to be the death of me yet."

"You've been saying that for years, Mom, and you're still as healthy as a horse." He grinned impishly at his mother while impatiently raking a hand across the tousled black hair falling across his forehead.

Ella was doing her best to look annoyed. "Well, it's a cinch I won't be after tonight. If I eat this stuff, the lining of my stomach will be fried and I'll have to take to my bed. Who's going to finish the cooking for Thanksgiving then?"

Sam laughed, knowing his mother had never taken to her bed in his life. She was one of the strongest and gentlest women he knew, even though she tried to hide her soft spots.

"Oh, we might talk Birdy Walker into coming over and doing a little cooking for you. Don't you think so, Kathleen?" he asked his sister, winking mischievously.

Kathleen tried not to smile as Ella raised a wooden spoon threateningly at her son. "Birdy Walker couldn't cook a piece of dry toast, much less a twenty-pound turkey! Now get out of here. Go wash. Supper's almost ready."

Still chuckling, Sam left the kitchen and crossed a wide breezeway. At the end of it a set of stairs led up to the bedrooms. He took them two at a time, just as he had since he'd turned ten and his legs had been long enough to accomplish the feat.

If there was one thing Sam had never been accused of, it was inconsistency. He supposed constancy had been bred into the Gallagher clan. This very farmhouse had been built more than a hundred years ago when Sam's Irish ancestors had helped put the railroad system through the state. His great-grandfather, Gorman Gallagher, had liked the Arkansas Valley so much he'd built a home along the river, and had decided to grow cotton instead of build railroads. Down through the years the old two-story structure had been added to and updated. It was the only home Sam had ever known or ever wanted.

When Sam came downstairs again, he found his father in the den, sitting at a rolltop desk. Reading glasses were perched on the end of his nose and a pencil was propped over one ear. S. T. Gallagher was a big man with an even bigger presence. He'd once had a head full of dark auburn hair, but now it was grizzled with gray. His name was Samuel Taylor, and Sam had been named for his father. But everyone called the older man S.T.

The elder Gallagher looked up as Sam entered the room. "It's about time you came back to the house. Did you get that piece on the disc welded?"

Sam crossed the room to stand by the fireplace. After spending the better part of the afternoon working in a cold barn, he needed to soak up heat from the roaring fire. "Yes. But I'm not going to promise how long it will hold once I start plowing with it again."

S.T. grunted. "Well, if we have to buy a new one, we'll just have to." The older man swiveled his chair toward Sam. "I was just going over last year's fertilizer bill. I hope you've come up with some way to whittle it down by spring planting time."

"I've been considering a couple of ideas that might help. A lot of the cost will eventually depend on fuel prices."

"And who the heck knows what they'll be," S.T. said, pulling the glasses from his nose and tossing them heedlessly onto the desk. "The way it looks it could be an expensive spring."

Ella's voice suddenly sounded from the doorway, attracting the men's attention. "I'm going to throw this food to the dogs if you two don't come now."

Chuckling, S.T. rose to his feet. "Guess we'd better get in there, or Jake and Leo are gonna get it."

The two men went out to the kitchen, where all the meals at the Gallagher home were eaten unless it was a special occasion. At those times the big formal dining room was opened up and the best china laid out. But tonight the four of them sat at a small table situated near a row of windows looking out over a section of land that followed the river. Presently the acreage was plowed under and was as barren-looking as the trees lining the riverbank.

"What is this?" S.T. asked as Ella passed around the pot of chili.

"Chili. Can't you tell by looking?"

The older man shook his head. "We just had stew last night. Can't this family have something that doesn't come out of a bowl?"

Ella gave him a dry look as she thrust a plate of hot corn bread at him. "S.T., we didn't have time to make a big meal. Kathleen and I are trying to get things ready for Thanksgiving. I'm making baked goods for the food baskets we're

distributing at church, and Kathleen wanted to add fresh
food to the canned goods she's donating to the troop drive."

He took the corn bread with a patient grin for his wife.
"I'm not griping, Ella. Lord knows we have plenty of food
around here to share with the needy. As long as I get one of
your famous mincemeat pies for Thanksgiving, then I guess
I can stand to eat chili tonight."

The smile Ella gave her husband was a loving one.
"Honey, I always cook you a mincemeat pie for Thanksgiving. This year won't be any different," she promised.

Sam began to fill his bowl with chili. "Well, I want pecan,
Mom. You still have some of those good Texas pecans, don't
you?"

Ella feigned a weary look, but the sparkle in her eyes said
exactly how much she was enjoying the fuss being made over
her cooking. "Yes, Sam, I have a five-pound bag. I'll bake
you a pecan pie. What about you, Kathleen? Is there a special pie you'd like?"

Kathleen smiled briefly. "No. I'm just going to enjoy us
all being together."

S.T. reached over and patted his daughter's cheek. "I'm
glad you're with us tonight, darlin'. There's no need for you
to stay in that big ole house of yours all by yourself. In fact,
I wish you'd sell the thing and move back home for good."

Kathleen shook her head. "You'd be sick of me in no
time, Dad. But I am considering selling the place. It . . . just
isn't the same since . . ."

Sam watched his sister's dark head drop and his heart
reached out to her. Kathleen was two years younger than he,
and two years older than their brother, Nick, who was away
in the army. For as long as he could remember he'd felt the
need to protect his sister. But he especially felt that way now.
Kathleen had lost her husband in a plane crash a year ago.
Since then Sam had watched his sister only pretend to be
herself.

Kathleen cleared her throat, then tried again. "Well, maybe after the holidays I'll list the house in the papers."

"I think Dad's right, Kathleen," Sam said. "You should move home with us. After all, when Mom and Dad leave next spring I'll be rattling around here all by myself."

"You're so sweet to want me, Sam. But I'm not going to make any firm decisions right now. After all, Mother has talked me into staying here through the holidays."

"Good, I'll put you to work feeding the hogs," Sam teased. "I hope you brought your rubber boots."

Ella shook her head. "You're not going to have Kathleen slopping around in that muddy hog pen. I'm going to need her help here in the kitchen. Besides, I haven't mentioned this to any of you yet, but I think we're going to have a houseguest."

Everyone at the table looked up in surprise. "A houseguest?" Kathleen echoed. "Mother, are you serious?"

Obviously enjoying the effect her announcement had made, Ella began to laugh. "Of course I'm serious."

S.T. began to crumble corn bread into his chili. "Okay, Ella, who have you invited to stay with us now? Allison?"

Allison Lee was a close neighbor who'd become a friend of the family in the past few months. No one at the table, least of all Sam, would be surprised to hear she would be a houseguest during Thanksgiving. Allison was an unwed mother, taking care of her child all by herself. If anyone needed help and friendship at Thanksgiving it would be she.

"No, Allison's going to be spending Thanksgiving with her grandmother, who's in the nursing home." With a smug little smile, Ella reached for her coffee cup. "I called Olivia Wescott yesterday. You know, she's back in the States now."

Ella's words froze Sam with shock, while across the table from him, Kathleen began clapping her hands gleefully.

"Olivia!" she squealed. "How long has she been back? How long will she stay?"

Ella held up a hand to halt her daughter's questions. "She's only been back a couple of weeks, I think. But when I asked her about Thanksgiving and found out she was going to be spending the holiday alone—well, I just had to insist that she spend it with us."

"And she's coming? Oh, this is so wonderful, Mother!" Kathleen was nearly bouncing on her seat. "When will she be here? I can't wait!"

Ella gave her daughter an indulgent smile and a pat on the hand. "Tomorrow or the next day. She wasn't sure when she could make it. But I told her we'd be watching for her."

A mist of happy tears filled Kathleen's eyes as she looked across the table at her brother. "Did you hear, Sam? Olivia's back from Africa."

Sam had heard, all right. The news had been like the blow of an ax falling in the middle of the dinner table. Olivia Wescott was back from Africa and coming here to the farm! Tomorrow! He couldn't believe it. He didn't want to believe it. Good Lord, didn't his mother realize what that would do to him?

"Yes, I heard," he finally managed to answer.

If his sister thought his lack of response unusual, she didn't show it. Suddenly turning to their mother, she began talking excitedly. Sam dipped his spoon into his chili and tried to eat. But the chili stuck in his throat like a tasteless piece of cotton.

No, his mother probably didn't know what Olivia's being here would do to him, Sam realized. No one in his family had known just how much Olivia had once meant to him. No one had known that for a while he'd thought he loved her. That she was the woman he wanted to spend the rest of his life with. But Olivia Wescott was cut from a different cloth. She'd walked away from him without so much as a backward glance, and as far as he knew she'd spent the past four years in Africa.

"She hasn't gotten married, has she?"

Kathleen's question jerked Sam out of his deep thoughts. He looked over to see his mother shrugging her shoulders. "If she's married she didn't mention it," Ella said. "And I doubt she would be bringing a husband with her without telling me first."

The chili that had stuck in Sam's throat had now become a ball of fire, making him reach for his water glass.

"You know," S.T. put in, "I just never could see that girl living over there in Africa. It has to be primitive. And her folks are rich enough to give her anything she wants."

From the corner of his eye, Sam could see Kathleen turn toward their father. "Olivia never cared about her parents' wealth. In fact, I think it always embarrassed her."

"Hell," S.T. said with a laugh, "I could take a little embarrassment like that, couldn't you, son?"

Sam knew his father was joking, but he couldn't find it in himself to be amused. "I suppose," he answered quietly.

"Dad, there are things in life other than money." Kathleen gently scolded her father.

"That's right, girl. I know all about them. Ella and you kids are worth more than any stack of money the Wescotts might have."

"Oh, it's just grand to be appreciated." Ella's tone was wry but the smile she gave her husband was sincere. Then she glanced at Kathleen. "Honey, I'm glad Olivia's coming has made you happy. You know, it's going to be like old times having you two girls here in the house again. Now if only Nick would call. If he's able to get leave, we'll all be together."

Sam couldn't take anymore. He pushed his bowl away and scraped his chair back from the table. "Mom, this chili is just too hot. I can't eat it."

Kathleen's mouth dropped open as she watched her brother leave the table.

"Samuel Taylor! What's the matter? Aren't you hungry?" his mother asked in disbelief.

"Ella, the boy just said the chili was too hot for him," S.T. told her.

The older woman shook her head at her husband. "S.T., he told me not more than half an hour ago to add another pepper to the pot!"

Ignoring both of them, Sam reached for the coat he'd left by the door and stepped out into the cold darkness. He had to be alone. He had to think. He had to convince himself that seeing Olivia Wescott again would mean nothing to him. Nothing at all.

Olivia slowed the car as a mixture of excitement and trepidation swept through her. Not more than twenty feet ahead of her was the Gallagher mailbox, and next to that, the entrance that led across a cattle guard and to the Gallagher farm.

Four years was a long time; she'd expected to see changes, but so far everything seemed achingly familiar. Turning the car into the graveled entrance, she started down a long dirt road that arced in a gentle curve toward the farmhouse in the distance.

Open fields lay on either side of the road. The remnants of some crop had been plowed under the loamy soil. Funny how easily Olivia could recall the last time she'd seen the place. Perfectly lined rows of spinach had grown for acres on end, and fields of hegari had nodded their yellow-white heads in the hot summer breeze.

The memory should have been a blurred one, especially since she'd only been on the Gallagher farm for a few short visits years ago. But nothing about her time here was blurred or forgotten, even though she sometimes wished it were.

Olivia had become friends with Kathleen Gallagher during their days together at the University of Arkansas in

Fayetteville. Days that seemed so long ago, Olivia thought. She'd been burning with fire and inspiration back then, so eager to go out and save the world.

She sighed deeply as the weight of the past few months settled even heavier on her shoulders. All that fire and determination hadn't made a difference in the end. The people in Africa were still starving by the thousands, just as they had been when she'd first gone there as a relief worker. Almost four years of her life had been given to the cause. And now she was wondering if it had all been in vain.

But Olivia's disillusionment seemed petty compared to what Kathleen had been through with losing her husband so tragically. She hoped her friend was coming to terms with the loss. She couldn't bear to think of Kathleen sick with grief. And if Olivia could lift her spirits, then it would be worth the awkwardness of seeing Sam again.

Since the road passed by the back of the house before curving around to the front, Olivia parked the car a few feet away from the rear gate.

No one had appeared to greet her by the time she'd pulled her bags from the trunk, so she shouldered her load and started to the house. Her knock at the back door went unanswered.

Shivering from the cold wind washing across the porch, Olivia tried the door and found it unlocked. "Kathleen? Ella?" she called as she stepped inside the warm kitchen. "Is anyone home?"

When no one answered, Olivia dumped her bags onto the floor to one side of the door, then walked to the center of the room. As she looked slowly around the large kitchen, she was transported back to the last time she'd visited the Gallagher farm.

Little had been altered in the big kitchen. It was still a bit cluttered, with all sorts of jars and canisters lining the shelves and cabinets. The curtains at the many windows had

been changed from the blue gingham Olivia remembered to
a print containing ducks and pigs with ribbons tied around
their necks. Black cast-iron cooking pots and skillets hung
from a work island in the middle of the room. A cookbook
lay open on the counter and Olivia could see where Ella had
written a comment to one side of a pumpkin pie recipe.

As Olivia turned away from the cookbook, she noticed a
note on the refrigerator door. Crossing to it, she read:

> Olivia, if you arrive before we get back, make yourself
> at home. There's coffee in the canister and brownies in
> a tin next to the bread box. Love, Kathleen.

Smiling to herself, Olivia began to gather the makings for
coffee. It was beginning to drip and fill the kitchen with a
rich aroma when she heard footsteps crossing the breezeway.

"Mom? Kathleen? Are you back?"

It was Sam's voice and Olivia's heart began to pound
fiercely in her chest. She opened her mouth to answer his
question, but the words refused to come. As his footsteps
grew nearer, she couldn't tear her gaze from the bat-wing
doors separating the kitchen and breezeway.

"Mother!"

"It—it's not Ella," Olivia finally said.

Chapter Two

Sam appeared at the doorway and Olivia felt her breath catch in her throat. All she could see was his head and shoulders, but it was enough to show that he was still as handsome and rugged looking as she remembered. His black hair had fallen in a thick, unruly shock across his forehead and a day's growth of beard covered his angular jaws and chin.

As he moved through the door Olivia's gaze traveled down the tall length of him. He was dressed in Levi's and a dark blue denim shirt with pearl snaps. He was still lean at the waist and hips, while his shoulders and arms were thickly corded with muscles. His physical appearance had always been impressive, but Olivia had to concede that the past four years had added to him. The youthful appearance she remembered had been replaced with a hardened edge of maturity that no doubt had turned many a woman's head.

His thin lips moved to a tight line as he spotted her standing at the kitchen cabinets. "Olivia," he said coolly.

"I smelled the coffee and thought it was Mom, or Kathleen."

Seeing him again after four long years had left her whole body trembling. The reaction surprised her. She'd thought she could look at him and be unaffected. It wasn't turning out that way at all.

"Hello, Sam," she said quietly, not certain that she could trust her voice to remain steady. God knew, nothing else felt steady about her.

He moved into the room and Olivia immediately spotted a bloody bandage wrapped around his left hand.

"You're hurt!" she gasped. Suddenly forgetting the awkward tension between them, she hurried over to him.

"It's nothing," he said grimly, thrusting his hand behind his back before she had a chance to take hold of it.

Frowning, Olivia shook her head at his foolish attitude. "Sam, you're bleeding. Let me see."

He brushed past her and walked over to the kitchen sink. "It's nothing, Olivia," he repeated coldly. "Just a little cut from a piece of tin."

Not to be daunted by his attitude, Olivia followed him. "If it's just a little cut, then you won't mind letting me put a bandage on it," she said, while reaching for the injured hand he was holding over the sink.

Blood was already dripping from the cloth he'd attempted to wrap around it, and Olivia knew he'd been underplaying the injury. Taking hold of his wrist, she began to unwrap the bandage. "I see you're still just as stubborn and strong-minded as you ever were," she said, praying her hands would remain steady and not betray the fact that her body was quaking.

Sam drew in a long breath as he tried to decide if it was the cut or Olivia that was making him feel light-headed. Even knowing she was coming hadn't prepared him for the swirl of emotions rushing through him at this moment.

"How did you do this anyway?" she asked, as she peeled the last of the soiled material from his fingers. Once it was removed, she began inspecting the wound. His ring and middle fingers had been sliced between the knuckles on the inside of his hand. Quickly she pushed the separated flesh back together and held it with a firm, steady pressure.

"I was nailing up a piece of corrugated iron on the back of the barn. The wind caught it and pulled it out of my grip. Are you—do you know what you're doing?"

Keeping a firm hold on his hand, she glanced up at him sharply. "Of course I know what I'm doing. I've had extensive first-aid training. Don't you remember?"

Remember? Good Lord, he remembered everything about her! Now, as his eyes clashed with her blue ones, he felt a knot tightening in his gut. She was so beautiful. Even with her face devoid of makeup it was rich with color. Her smooth complexion had been tanned deeply by the hot African sun, making her blue eyes appear startling in contrast. Her platinum blond hair was pulled back and tied at her nape with a wide pink ribbon. The color matched the pink flush on her cheeks and the soft angora sweater she was wearing. He didn't have to reach out and touch her face to know that it would be as soft as it looked. He didn't have to kiss her to know that her full lips would be as warm and sweet as he remembered. It was all there for him to see.

"You should have been wearing gloves," she said, hoping she didn't sound as breathless as she felt.

"I was," he told her, unable to tear his eyes away from hers. The touch of her hands was like a sweet memory come back to haunt him. At the moment he couldn't decide if he wanted to push her away or jerk her into his arms.

Feeling a wave of heat wash through her, Olivia forced her gaze away from his and back to his injured hand. After carefully lifting the pressure of her fingers, she watched the cut for a few moments to make sure the bleeding had stopped. "How long has it been since you've had a tetanus shot?"

"About a month ago—Nurse Wescott," he tacked on dryly.

She stabbed him with a sidelong glance. "Too bad. I would have enjoyed jabbing you with a needle."

He gave her a stony look before she turned her attention back to his fingers. "If you'll tell me where I can find a first-aid kit I'll wrap this up for you."

Sam wished he could tell her to leave him alone, but they both knew he needed her help. With only one hand, he could never manage to bandage the fingers himself. Why in hell did Kathleen and his mother have to be gone now?

"There's one in the cabinet. Over to your left," he said, motioning with a nod of his head.

Olivia went to find it. While she searched through the odds and ends of the cabinet she could feel his eyes on her. She wondered what was going through his mind. Was he thinking the same erotic thoughts she was thinking?

"I suppose you were angry with your mother for inviting me here for Thanksgiving?" she asked, returning to his side with the first-aid box.

Damn right, he'd been angry, he thought. He'd wanted to be furious with his mother for inviting Olivia to the farm. But his real anger was directed at himself. He shouldn't care whether Olivia was here or still in Africa. It shouldn't matter to him. And he hated himself because it did.

Her head was bent as she searched through the rolls of cotton and gauze. Sam couldn't stop himself from studying the crown of her head and the way the kitchen light picked up the shine in her hair. She was the only woman he'd ever known with hair the color of white-hot sunshine. He'd seen color close to it on children who played outdoors during the summertime, and he'd seen a pitiful semblance of it on other women who attempted to get it from a bottle. But Olivia was a natural. In more ways than one, he thought grimly.

"Mom obviously wanted you here," he finally said. "And I wasn't about to put up a fuss and ruin my family's holiday."

"But you wanted to, right?" she persisted.

"I wanted to, but I didn't. Okay?"

Olivia didn't know why anything he said should matter to her, but it did. After applying antiseptic to the cuts, she began to wrap clean gauze around each finger. "While I was still in Africa I wrote your mother and told her to contact me when I got back to the States. I'd been worried about Kathleen. She hadn't written to me since—well, since after her letter explaining Greg's death. I was afraid...well, she sounded so depressed I didn't know what was happening with her."

Sam could understand that. The whole family had been worried about Kathleen's state of mind ever since the accident that had taken her husband's life.

When Sam didn't say anything, Olivia felt as if she had to go on, to try to make him understand why she'd had to come back. "I never expected Ella to invite me here. But when she did I...felt like Kathleen needed to see me. And that any differences you and I had in the past could be put aside for her sake."

Maybe Kathleen did need to see her old friend. But that didn't mean Sam did. He had no desire to be reminded of the pain and rejection Olivia Wescott had put him through.

"Is that what we had, Olivia? Differences?"

His voice was sharp and cutting. Olivia's eyes roamed his face, searching for the strong, yet gentle man she used to know.

"I once believed we had more than that," she said quietly.

"Sure you did," he said, gritting his teeth. "I'm just thankful to God my family doesn't know what really went on between us. At least you saved me that humiliation."

Humiliation? Had the closeness they'd once shared been a humiliation to him? The idea was unbelievably painful to her. Olivia looked up at him, her blue eyes hardened with bitterness. "I'm sorry that my infatuation with you was so humiliating."

So she was calling it infatuation now, Sam thought. He could remember a time when she'd sworn it was love. A mocking twist moved his lips. "I don't think you're sorry, Olivia. Not about anything."

Did he want her to be sorry? she wondered wildly. Sorry that she'd turned down his proposal of marriage? The question and his sarcasm was too much for Olivia to handle. She tried her best to ignore him and focus her attention on wrapping his fingers.

Even though she was shaking inside, she somehow managed to keep her hands steady as she wrapped the gauze around the cut. Once she decided the bandage was thick enough, she tied the free ends together, then covered them with a piece of white tape. "There. That should hold it awhile. But in my opinion it needs stitches."

"I didn't ask for your opinion, or your services," he said tightly.

She glanced up at him, her features hard as stone. "No, you didn't, did you? But if it will make you feel any better, you can pay me. After all, we both know how much you hate charity. You never could understand one person helping another simply out of need."

His eyes suddenly blazed with anger. Before Olivia realized his intentions, his uninjured hand had closed in a tight grip around her upper arm.

"Charity had nothing to do with you and me," he said roughly, his face dipping close to hers.

"You and me. Was there ever really a you and me, Sam?" she asked, her voice going suddenly soft.

His mind tried to reason out her question, but as his eyes fastened on her soft, moist lips, he ceased to think. With a tug of his hand he pulled her against his chest.

As Olivia struggled to push away from him, his face blurred her vision. The next thing she knew his mouth was on hers. Hot, forceful, punishing.

With a shocked whimper, Olivia's hands came up to push him away. She didn't want him like this. She didn't want him in any capacity, she thought wildly.

Until that moment Sam had been blinded with the need to punish her, but her soft, sweet lips were quickly changing that particular need to an entirely different one. Without realizing it, the pressure of his mouth eased, his hand lifted from her arm to slide up the side of her neck and cup her jaw.

Olivia didn't know exactly how or what had happened, but suddenly everything had changed. Her head was lying in the crook of his arm, his lips were moving over hers in a slow, delicious kiss that was making her legs weak, her hands were clinging to his shoulders.

From somewhere outside came the sound of a car door slamming, then another. Hearing it, Sam lifted his head, and for a moment he looked into Olivia's blue eyes. They were heavy lidded and clouded with desire. For one wild moment he wanted to forget everything and kiss her again.

"Sam." The name slipped softly from her parted lips as her eyes pleaded with him to let her go, to understand, to forgive.

It wasn't until voices and footsteps were heard on the porch that Sam released his hold on her and moved a few steps away. By then Olivia was dazed and trembling from head to foot. How in heaven's name was she going to face

Ella and Kathleen? She knew her face must be flushed, her lips swollen.

Desperately she turned from him and drew in a long, steadying breath. Behind her she heard Sam's footsteps cross the room, and then the sound of the door being opened.

"It's about time you two got back," he said gruffly as Ella and Kathleen pushed past him.

"Olivia!" With a squeal of joy Kathleen raced across the room and flung her arms around her friend. "Oh, my goodness, you look so beautiful! Look at her, Mother!"

Ella dropped the bags of groceries she was carrying at Sam's feet and rushed over to the two women. "Oh, Livvy honey, I'm so glad you're here!" She drew Olivia against her breast and hugged her tightly.

Sam felt some strange, inexplicable feeling wash over him as he watched his mother wipe at the tears on her cheeks. Even though Ella knew Olivia only from her few short visits to the farm, his mother loved her like a daughter. Kathleen loved her, too. Olivia had that way about her, he thought—of making a person love her on first sight. He'd been a victim of her charm, too, he thought bitterly. But not anymore. Now he knew she wasn't the compassionate woman she pretended to be. A compassionate woman couldn't walk away from the man she loved. Not for any reason.

"We had to make a trip into town," Kathleen explained. "Mother insisted she needed fresh sage for the Thanksgiving stuffing. How long have you been here? Did Sam show you where to put your things?"

"I smell coffee. Have you had a cup?" Ella asked before Olivia could open her mouth to answer the first string of questions.

"Er, no. Sam was—" Olivia started, only to stop as Kathleen interrupted her.

"Sam! What happened to your hand?" Kathleen demanded as she caught sight of her brother's bandaged fingers.

Grimacing, he turned away from the women and headed to the coffeepot. "Nothing much. Olivia's the nurse. She can tell you."

Color stung her cheeks as Kathleen and Ella turned their questioning looks back to her. "He cut it on a piece of tin. I just happened to arrive in time to bandage it for him. I told him he needs stitches, but I don't think he trusts my opinion."

Kathleen whirled on her brother. "Sam, if you need stitches, you must drive over to the clinic!"

"Stitches, hell!" he barked, "I've had bug bites worse than this."

Ella shook her head with wry resignation. "Kathleen, don't badger your brother. He's a grown man—he ought to know if he needs medical attention or not."

Olivia watched Sam splash coffee into a thick brown cup. His face had grown oddly pale. She didn't know if it was from his injury or the heated exchange she'd had with him. Either way it was obvious he was still angry with her or himself. Probably both, she decided. Moreover, Olivia was still trying to figure out why he'd kissed her. Why, for a few sweet moments, it had felt like nothing had changed between them.

"Mom," Sam said, forcing patience into his voice, "has Dad come back from the feed store yet?"

"He wasn't out there when we drove up," she answered.

Deciding her brother wasn't seriously injured, Kathleen turned back to Olivia. Her face was wreathed in smiles as she grabbed her friend by the hand. "Come sit at the table, Olivia. I'll get us coffee and brownies. You're going to have some, too, aren't you, Mother?"

The older woman motioned for them to go ahead without her. "I'll be with you as soon as I put the groceries away."

Sam quickly drained the last of his coffee and headed toward the door. "I've got work to do," he said abruptly, stopping long enough at the door to shrug into a brown work coat. "I'll see you all at supper."

The door shut behind him, and Kathleen stared at it with a puzzled expression. "Well, I wonder what he's in such a snit about? It's not like him to be so short."

"I expect his hand is hurting." Ella spoke as she pushed a box of dry cereal onto a shelf. "You know how men are— it's not macho to admit you might need a painkiller."

Kathleen shrugged as she began to gather cups and saucers and place them on an enameled tray. "You're probably right. But I thought he'd at least stay and talk with Olivia a few minutes. The man drives himself too much as it is. He seems to forget it's wintertime. This *is* a farmer's time to rest."

"His hand *was* cut deeply," Olivia said in hopes of explaining Sam's unusual behavior. Lord only knew what the two women would have thought if they'd walked in moments earlier to find them kissing. "I'm sure he doesn't feel like talking to anyone right now."

Thankfully, Kathleen left it at that, and for the next half hour the three women chatted at length over coffee and brownies. Ella and Kathleen wanted to know as much as Olivia could tell them about her job in Africa. She tried to answer their questions with as much enthusiasm as she could. But her thoughts weren't really on the conversation.

Her encounter with Sam had left her shaken, and try as she might, she couldn't get him out of her mind. The kiss they had exchanged was crazy! Senseless! It should never have happened. So why had it? she asked herself, and why couldn't she forget it?

"Olivia, if you've had enough coffee, let's go upstairs and I'll show you where to put your things," Kathleen suggested.

Olivia pushed her empty cup to one side and rose from the table. "I've had plenty," she assured Kathleen, reaching for the bags she'd left by the door.

Kathleen quickly took one of them from Olivia and hefted the strap over her shoulder. "My dear, I know that you're always taking care of others, but the ceiling won't fall in if someone does something for you."

Olivia feigned a worried look and glanced up at the ceiling. "Are you sure?"

Kathleen laughed and Ella said, "Olivia, by the time we tie you up in this kitchen for a few days, you'll be wanting to go back to Africa."

Moments later, as the two women climbed the stairs, Kathleen glanced over at Olivia. "Mother is taking it for granted that you are returning to Africa. Are you ... going back?"

That was a question that had haunted Olivia for the past several months. Reality told her to face the facts. She would never be going back to Africa. But there was another part of her that wasn't quite ready to accept the finality of it. "Well, not anytime soon. I've been ill and the doctors sent me to the States to recuperate."

Kathleen was suddenly all concern. "Oh? I hope it's not anything too serious."

Olivia smiled wanly. "No. Just a tropical bug I picked up. Nothing that lots of rest and antibiotics won't cure."

Kathleen sighed with obvious relief. "Thank goodness. You had me worried there for a minute."

At the landing, they turned to the left and Kathleen pushed open a bedroom door. Olivia followed her through it.

"Mom and I fixed this room for you. I hope it has everything you need."

Olivia smiled as she looked around at the papered walls done in tiny flowers. The bed, which had an iron railed headboard painted in white, was covered with a lemon-colored spread that matched the priscillas at the windows. "Are you kidding? This is luxury compared to the places I've been living in," she said.

"I know, but your parents' place in Hot Springs is so fancy, so—" Kathleen broke off as a tight look spread over Olivia's face.

"Impersonal," Olivia finished for her. "That's not me anymore, Kathleen. It never really was." She smiled gently to reassure her friend. "I'm not living with them now, anyway. I've taken an apartment in Little Rock."

Frowning, Kathleen placed the bag she'd been carrying on the foot of the bed. "You really expect to be here in the States that long? Olivia, are you telling me the truth about your illness?"

Olivia dumped the bag she was holding onto the bed with the others. "Kathleen," she scolded lightly. "Quit fretting. Of course I told you the truth. I'll be fine. I just needed a place to stay."

Which was true enough, Olivia thought. After a little rest and medication her body would be back to normal. It was her heart and spirit that was having the real problem. A few minutes ago, as they had talked over coffee, Ella and Kathleen had kept saying how exciting it must be for her to work in a foreign country and do things that others only dream about doing.

Maybe it had been exciting in those first few weeks, when Olivia's spirits had been on fire to help the suffering people in the world. But once she'd been faced with the devastating reality of starvation, the excitement had quickly turned to grim determination. Now, after four years, and with hardly any progress to show for it, she felt totally defeated.

Looking back at Kathleen she said, "I know this sounds crazy, Kathleen, but I feel guilty being here in the States. I know there are people back in Africa who are dying...." And no matter how much she helped, the dying never stopped. She'd reached the point where she couldn't take anymore. But how could she tell Kathleen that now? Her friend had enough problems of her own to deal with.

Kathleen walked over and put her arm around Olivia's slender shoulders. "Livvy," she said gently, "you can't carry such a burden with you day in, day out. It isn't selfish of you to take time off for yourself. Besides, I'm the selfish one here. I've been wanting to see you so badly."

Olivia reached for the other woman's hand and gave it an affectionate tug. "And I've been wanting to see you, too. You can't imagine how shocked I was to get your letter about Greg. It's been nearly a year now since the plane crash, hasn't it?"

Kathleen nodded and moved away from her. "Yes, last winter," she said, her voice growing distant. "There was a snowstorm going on. He was flying through the Boston Mountains and apparently lost visibility."

"I'm so sorry things turned out like they did, Kathleen. You deserve to be happy."

"Happy," Kathleen murmured as she tried to muster a brave smile. "Yes, I'm going to be happy. I have to believe that." Her smile suddenly turned to an impish one. "But right now I'd settle for a tan like yours. You're as brown as a nut! I'd have to lay in a tanning bed for hours to look like that."

Olivia laughed. "It's your Irish complexion. I'll bet you never knew how much I envied your milk white skin and dark hair."

Kathleen rolled her eyes in disbelief. "And you a true, blue-eyed blonde? The guys in college were all dying to date you. Remember?"

Olivia remembered that the only guy she'd ever wanted was Sam Gallagher. But in the end he'd considered the farm much more important than her, or her ideals.

Unzipping one of the bags, Olivia began to pull out several pieces of neatly folded clothing. "You've had a memory warp, my dear Kathleen. You were the one who had all the guys tongue-tied."

Laughing, Kathleen plopped down on the edge of the bed. "Oh? Is that why I only had one invitation to every five of yours? They were too tongue-tied to ask me?"

With a soft chuckle, Olivia carried a handful of toiletries over to a small dressing table. "Your sultry beauty intimidated them. Remember that guy who broke out in hives every time he danced with you?"

"Remember? Are you kidding?" Kathleen giggled. "He was painfully shy, and me, believing I could cure him of it in one night, forced him to dance nearly every dance with me. Poor thing, he probably still cringes when he thinks about it. He itched and scratched for two days afterward."

The smile fell from Olivia's face. "I don't suppose Sam has come close to marrying? I thought...that maybe he'd have a family by now."

Kathleen let out something close to a snort. "He hasn't even come close. There was a schoolteacher named Susan Williams that he saw a few times, but that was over almost before it began. I've just about given up on him."

Olivia didn't know if she was relieved or saddened to learn that Sam was avoiding women. Either way, she refused to believe that she was the reason he was shying away from marriage. The man was selfish and narrow-minded. He probably couldn't find a woman he felt was worthy of him.

"Well," she said, careful to keep her voice light, "from what I remember of Sam, he has a mind of his own. And if he's as serious-minded as he used to be, he'd never date just for the sake of dating."

"You're probably right," Kathleen said, then laughed a bit sheepishly. "You know, I used to think that maybe you and he would get together somehow. I guess it was just wishful thinking on my part. You know, my brother and my best friend. Crazy, huh?"

Olivia felt frozen inside. "Yeah, that's pretty crazy. If I was the last woman on earth, Sam would run from me."

A puzzled frown came over Kathleen's face. "Why do you say that? Sam always liked you. Why, when you spent those three weeks with me after graduation, you and Sam spent a lot of time together. I could tell he was beginning to like you."

Like her, Olivia silently repeated. Like was such a meek emotion compared to what she'd felt for him. During those three weeks she'd spent here on the farm, she'd fallen head over heels in love with Sam Gallagher. And when he'd proposed to her, she'd desperately wanted to say yes. But she'd already committed herself to the job in Africa. It was what she'd trained for, what she lived for. But Sam hadn't been able to understand her need to go there. He hadn't wanted to understand. It had been marriage his way or no marriage at all. She'd been so hurt and angry at his ultimatum that she'd left the farm, packed up everything she needed from her home in Hot Springs and departed for Africa without saying another word to Sam Gallagher.

Olivia hoped the smile on her face wasn't as bitter as it felt. "Maybe he did. But I think Sam prefers old-fashioned women. If he ever marries, it will be to someone who agrees with everything he says, and kisses the ground he walks on."

Kathleen was obviously amazed at Olivia's opinion of her brother. "Good Lord! If that's the case, I hope he never marries. I couldn't stand having a timid, browbeaten sister-in-law.''

To be honest, Olivia couldn't stand to think of Sam having a timid, kowtowing wife, either. He was a strong man. He needed an equally strong woman. Maybe someday he'd realize that.

"Well, what about Nick?" Olivia asked, deciding she'd heard enough about Sam Gallagher's love life, or the lack of it. "Does he still like women?"

The question had Kathleen laughing uproariously. "Sit down, Olivia, we have a couple of hours before dinner. That might be long enough to tell you about a few of the women Nick writes home about.''

Chapter Three

By suppertime Sam was in a better frame of mind. He showered and changed into clean jeans and a pale blue cotton shirt, then combed his wet hair back with his good hand. He needed to shave but he wasn't going to do it tonight and have Olivia thinking he'd shaved just for her.

Olivia. It was still hard to believe she was here and would be for at least another three days. Obviously he couldn't avoid her all that time. So there was nothing left to do but face her head-on. He would think of it as an exorcism, one that had been too long in coming.

When he went down for supper, everyone was in the den. His mother was perched on his father's knee, while Kathleen and Olivia were sharing the couch. Sam walked over to the fireplace and turned his back to his flames.

"How's your hand, son?" S.T. asked him. "Olivia says it was a pretty deep gash."

Sam couldn't stop his gaze from crossing the room to Olivia. Her chin lifted a fraction as she looked back at him. "Olivia exaggerated," he told his father. "It'll be fine."

"We're having a drink, Sam. Why don't you get yourself something?" his mother suggested. "There's brandy or wine."

Sam's brows lifted in wry speculation. "Are we celebrating? You rarely have spirits in the house."

Ella frowned at her son. "I do when the occasion warrants it. And of course we're celebrating. It's nearly Thanksgiving. My family is intact and Olivia is back from Africa for a visit. That more than deserves a toast."

"Here, here," S.T. said in his boisterous voice. "And your mama has cooked a stack of short ribs tonight. I'm gonna kiss her all over the face for that."

Ella pushed a hand against his chest to ward off any advances he might try to make. "Not in front of the children," she said with a primness that was so obviously feigned everyone in the room laughed.

"These children are of age," S.T. assured her. "They won't mind."

Before he could make his move, Ella jumped up from his knee. "Sam, if you don't want a drink, let's go in to supper before everything gets cold."

"I'll vote for that," Kathleen said. "I'm hungry and I know Olivia must be. She didn't eat lunch on her drive from Little Rock."

"That's a long drive, Olivia," S.T. said. "You should have stopped for a break."

Olivia felt warmed by S.T.'s concern, but then the older Gallagher had always been especially kind to her during her visits to the farm. He was like the father she'd always wanted, and the exact opposite from the one she had.

"I made it just fine," she assured him. "Although it does seem strange driving on the opposite side of the highway again," she added.

"I didn't realize you'd had the opportunity to drive that much over in Ethiopia," Kathleen commented.

"Yes, I drove every day. Mostly Jeeps and four-wheel-drive vehicles. There are fairly updated roads around Addis Ababa, where our headquarters are located. But there're only dirt tracks out in the bush. You drive wherever you can."

Sam had often wondered what Olivia's day-to-day life was like. Hundreds of times he'd tried to imagine her working in the sweltering heat, taking sponge baths out of a dishpan and sleeping on a hard, narrow cot. But it was an image of her that he could never quite accept. She was a petite, delicately built woman, one who was too gentle, too beautiful to live in such a rough way.

Four years ago, when Olivia had first told Sam what she planned to do with her life, he hadn't taken her seriously. He'd found it unbelievable that she would leave her home, her family and, most of all, him behind. He'd thought she loved him. He'd thought he was more important to her than people in a country thousands of miles away. She'd proved him wrong when she'd turned down his proposal and left for Africa in spite of his wish to keep her on the farm with him.

"Why aren't we eating in the dining room?" Sam asked as everyone took their seats at the kitchen table. His brown eyes turned to Olivia, who was easing onto the seat next to him. "Olivia's company, after all," he added.

His words stung her. Just as he'd meant them to. She knew he was reminding her that she wasn't a true member of this family, and that *he* hadn't invited her for a visit.

When Olivia had decided to accept Ella's invitation, she'd expected Sam to treat her coolly. She'd thought she could handle it, at least for Kathleen's sake. But now that she was here on the farm, facing him in the flesh, she was afraid the days ahead were going to rip her apart emotionally.

"I like to think of myself as family, Sam." In spite of what you might think of me, she added silently.

Sam didn't reply. He knew how his family felt about Olivia. From the first time Kathleen had brought her home for a weekend, they'd all fallen in love with her. Himself included. Olivia had known that, too, he thought bitterly. But, by damn, he was determined to show her it was far from that way now.

Dinner turned out to be more pleasant than Olivia had first thought it might be. The older Gallaghers kept the conversation flowing as they tried to catch Olivia up on four years of news that had happened while she'd been away.

During the meal, she'd expected Sam to throw a few cutting words her way. Instead he was noticeably quiet, hardly saying anything unless a question was put to him directly. Olivia hoped the rest of the family put his behavior down to his cut hand instead of to her arrival. She knew how special Thanksgiving was to the Gallagher family. She certainly didn't want to spoil this time when they planned to gather and celebrate.

"When will your family be back in Hot Springs?" Ella asked Olivia sometime later, when everyone was having coffee in the den.

S.T. had built up the fire and Olivia had taken a seat on the floor by the hearth. Now she looked over at the older woman, who was knitting a sweater out of cherry red yarn. "They won't return from Florida until sometime in January. That's when the horse racing begins at Oaklawn," she explained.

"What are you going to do for Christmas, Olivia?" Kathleen spoke up hopefully. "Couldn't you stay with us until then?"

Olivia could feel Sam's hooded gaze turn on her, and even though he was sitting several feet away in a stuffed armchair, she could feel the heat of his brown eyes boring into her, striking a spark inside of her that she was trying her best to ignore.

"Oh, Kathleen, that's too far ahead for me to commit myself."

Kathleen looked disappointed. Sam, on the other hand, looked relieved. Olivia tried not to think about how glad he would be to see her leave after Thanksgiving. And she knew, probably just as he did, that she would never return. Coming back and meeting Sam's bitter wrath head-on had proved to her that the old adage about going home again was true.

"Well, surely you'd like to be here for Christmas?" Kathleen went on. "How would you celebrate if you were in Africa?"

Olivia smiled wryly at Kathleen's question. "I don't want to dampen your holiday spirit, Kathleen, but we've always been too busy trying to keep people alive to have time to celebrate. We usually have a church service on Christmas Eve and a small exchange of gifts at breakfast the next morning."

S.T. looked up from his evening newspaper. "Don't be selfish, sis," he said to Kathleen, just as he had when she was a child, asking for the impossible. "Olivia is here now. Be satisfied with that."

Kathleen gave her daddy the same adoring smile she'd given him since she'd been able to sit on his knee, then looked back to Olivia. "Okay, I won't press you, Olivia. But it would be nice. I just hope Nick gets to stay through the holidays. He'll liven things up around here. There's hardly ever a moment he isn't joking or laughing."

Olivia nodded her agreement. "The one time I met him, he seemed like a fun-loving guy."

Sam tossed his sister a droll look. "Thanks, Kathleen, for pointing out how boring I am."

Kathleen looked at him with mild surprise. "Who said anything about you being boring? You've been downright grouchy today."

Sam grimaced as he lifted his coffee cup to his lips. He knew Kathleen was right. He wasn't acting himself, but seeing Olivia again had knocked the wind out of him. He hadn't expected it to, but it had. And why in heaven's name he'd kissed her, he didn't know. A complete lapse of sanity, he supposed. But the way she'd touched him, the way she'd looked at him had set him on fire. Even now he couldn't ignore the heat that ignited each time he looked at her.

"Kathleen, a man is entitled to be a little grouchy once in a while," Sam replied. "Besides, I haven't noticed you being the life of the party here lately."

Olivia watched Kathleen's expression turn to a lifeless mask, then glanced at Sam, wondering how the man could be so heartless.

Sam wished he could take the words back as soon as he said them. But from the expression on his sister's face, he knew the damage had already been done. Well, he thought with a weary sigh, it was past time for the whole family to stop handling Kathleen with kid gloves. She'd never get over her grief if they continually tried to cushion her. Yet he doubted Olivia agreed with his thinking. At the moment she looked like she could run a knife through him.

Ella suddenly broke the silence. "Why don't we put a movie in the VCR? I'm sure Olivia isn't caught up on any of the newer movies."

Grateful for anything to get her thoughts off Sam, Olivia said, "I never get to see movies at all. I'd love to see one."

"Good," Ella said without looking up from her knitting needles. "Kathleen, you and Olivia pick something out, will you?"

From behind his newspaper, S.T. said, "Let's see *The Naked Spur.*"

"Dad, we've seen *The Naked Spur* so many times I can recite every word Jimmy Stewart says," Kathleen told him. "Olivia needs to see something soft and romantic. It wouldn't hurt Sam, either,'' she tacked on, her impish humor quickly returning.

Sam put his coffee cup to one side and rose to his feet. He'd promised himself he wouldn't deliberately avoid Olivia, but watching a love story in the same room with her would be utter torture for him. "Sorry, sis, I'm going up to my room. It's been a long day and to be honest, my hand is throbbing."

Suddenly contrite, Kathleen went over to her brother and slipped an arm around his waist. "No, I'm sorry, Sam. Why don't you take something for your hand before you go upstairs?''

With a shake of his head, he leaned down and kissed his sister's cheek. "I'll be fine. You and Olivia enjoy your movie and I'll see you in the morning."

Hours later, Sam was still tossing from one side of the oak four-poster to the other. Through a window by the bed, he could see the clear night sky strung with stars. Just above the cottonwoods that lined the riverbank hung a sliver of a moon. He'd been gazing at it for some time now, wondering if Olivia had seen it before turning in.

He knew she was across the hall from him in her own bedroom. He'd heard her footsteps when she'd come upstairs, her whispered good-night to Kathleen, then the soft click of her door closing.

Turning onto his side, he tried to move his bandaged hand to a more comfortable position and winced as another pain shot through it. Olivia had probably been right about it needing stitches. But it wasn't the ache in his hand that was keeping him awake. It was Olivia. The way she looked, the way she smelled and the way she'd felt when he'd taken her into his arms. It was all in his head, going round and round, making him remember things he shouldn't be remembering.

He didn't know why this fixation for Olivia Wescott was still with him. She was like one of those recurring tropical fevers for which there was no remedy. They left a man weak and disoriented. Just like Olivia would leave him if he didn't watch his step, he thought grimly.

Muttering an oath under his breath, he tossed back the covers and swung his legs over the side of the bed. With any luck he'd find some leftovers in the kitchen, he thought, as he pulled on his jeans.

Across the hall, Olivia heard Sam the moment he came out of his room, and then his footsteps as he descended the stairs two at a time.

Obviously he couldn't sleep. Neither could she. But it was her memories keeping her awake, whereas it was probably Sam's injured hand that was disturbing him. Just the idea that his pain had worsened was enough to make Olivia toss back the covers and reach for her robe.

Except for a small light on the hood of the range, the kitchen was dark when Olivia entered it a few moments later. Sam was standing next to the cabinets, pulling a piece of clear cellophane from a plate of leftover ribs.

She moved toward him, careful not to stumble over anything in the darkness.

Sam lifted his head, surprise registering on his face when he saw that it was Olivia.

"Olivia? What are you doing down here?"

She stopped a step or two away from him and leaned her hip against the cabinet counter. "I was afraid your hand was giving you problems," she said in a hushed tone. "Is it all right?"

He glanced momentarily at his bandaged fingers, then over to her. The faint light from the range illuminated her face and the fall of blond hair caressing the tops of her shoulders. She was wearing something soft and flimsy. It was the color of a ripe peach and came to a V at the top of her breasts. He could see that the exposed skin was as brown as her face, and he wondered what he would find if he pushed the robe aside. Would her breasts be just as tanned? Or would they be milky white, the tips dusky pink?

Quickly, in an effort to halt his erotic thoughts, he looked away from her and said, "The hand is okay. I took a couple of aspirins about an hour ago."

Olivia drew in a long breath as her eyes glided over his bare torso. He was beautifully made, his chest and arms strongly muscled, his waist lean and trim. Fine black hair dusted his chest and grew in a tempting circle around each flat nipple.

In her work Olivia had seen many men without shirts and had never had a second thought about it. But seeing Sam in an undressed state was something quite different. Especially in the quiet darkness.

"Why aren't you asleep?" he asked, setting the plate of ribs on the stove.

Olivia's arms folded protectively against her waist. "I suppose it's the time change. My system thinks it should be daylight," she said. She wasn't about to tell him that he was the real reason she'd tossed and turned in bed for the past two hours. He wouldn't believe it anyway, she thought. Sam Gallagher believed she was a selfish woman who'd never really loved him. And maybe that was for the best, she thought sadly. It would probably just complicate things even more if he knew how much she actually *had* loved him.

"Africa is half a world away. You went to a lot of trouble to come back just for a visit."

Olivia studied his face, wondering exactly how much he knew about her return to the States. Obviously Kathleen hadn't told him that she'd been ill, thank God. Four years ago he'd predicted she would come back from Africa with nothing but a broken back and a broken spirit. That hadn't turned out to be exactly the truth, but it was so close that it hurt. And it was something she wasn't about to let Sam know.

"After four years I think anyone deserves a vacation. To visit family and friends." She was trying her best to sound casual, but that was very hard to do when she had to keep reminding herself to breathe.

"If I heard right earlier tonight, your parents aren't even home to visit," he said a bit skeptically.

"No, they aren't. But I will see them later on."

Her eyes slipped away from his, but not before he saw dark shadows flicker in the blue depths. From what Olivia had told him in the past, she wasn't close to her parents, nor they to her. The Wescotts traveled in the rich social circles of the business world. They'd never accepted, as far as Sam knew, that their only child wasn't a social flower, but instead a woman who worked in squalid conditions.

Unlike the Wescotts, Sam had understood when Olivia had told him that money or social standing couldn't make her happy. But he hadn't been able to understand that going halfway around the world, and away from him, would.

"What about the man you left behind? How did he take being left alone on the holidays?"

She looked at him blankly. "Man?"

Sam's features were suddenly twisted with mockery. "Yeah, you know. Like a sweetheart. A lover. Surely you have one of those, don't you?"

The question was a taunt and Olivia gritted her teeth as she tried to hold on to her composure. "You're not really interested in that, or me, Sam. So I really see no point in wasting my breath to answer."

He moved a step closer. Olivia began to tremble as he reached out and ran his forefinger along the neckline of her robe.

"How do you know I'm not interested?" he asked, the innocent arch of his brows contrasting oddly with the mocking sarcasm in his voice.

Olivia desperately wanted to step back and away from his touch. But to do so would be admitting that his touch still had the power to affect her. Her eyes lifted defiantly to meet his. "When you returned my unopened letters, your feelings were spelled out loud and clear, Sam. I realized then that you'd never really been interested in me. Not as a wife."

The gentle movement of his fingers stilled against her skin. Heat washed through Olivia's body, leaving her legs weak, her mind spinning. She wanted to reach up and slap his hand away. Anything to end the torment his touch was causing her.

"I didn't want a letter from you, Olivia. I wanted you. But that hardly mattered to you, did it? You were too busy trying to prove to your parents, and the world, that you weren't a spoiled little rich girl."

She wasn't ready for the awful accusation in his voice. She'd never expected his anger to last. Four years was a long time. She'd thought all that had been put in the past by both of them. Obviously it hadn't been. She still turned to putty when he touched her, and he was still blaming her for the way their brief romance had ended.

Suddenly Olivia wished she'd never came back. Even seeing Kathleen and the rest of the Gallaghers wasn't worth this torture of tearing open past wounds.

"I went to Africa to help starving people, Sam. Not to prove something, as you seem to think."

His mocking snort of disbelief tore at Olivia's heart.

"Well, you proved something to me," Sam told her. "You proved that you didn't give a damn about me, or the fact that I wanted you to be my wife."

Earlier, Olivia had been determined not to back down from him, but she could no longer take his bitter anger.

Spinning on her heel, she turned to leave the room. However, Sam caught hold of her arm before she could take one step.

"Is that the way you still deal with things, Olivia? Run from them?"

The question had her whirling back to face him. "I don't know how you can talk to me like this," she whispered fiercely. "I can't understand why you'd even want to!"

Why did he? he asked himself. Because every time he looked at Olivia he thought of the last night he'd seen her. The two of them had argued viciously about the idea of her going abroad to work. They had come close to making love. Yet two days later she'd left for Africa as though he'd never meant anything to her. He'd felt used and discarded, and he'd hated her for breaking his heart.

"Maybe I'm just not a forgiving man, Olivia." Dropping her arm as though it were poison, he brushed past her and started out of the room.

Dazed, Olivia stared after him. So he thought *she* needed forgiving? The man was crazy!

Olivia caught up to him in the breezeway. The moment she touched his arm, he came to an abrupt halt. He kept his back to her.

"Don't walk away from me like that, Sam Gallagher!" she ordered under her breath. "You talk about forgiving, but you don't bother to ask me if I've forgiven you. And if you're the slightest bit curious, the answer is no. I haven't forgiven you. God knows, I've tried. And I thought I had— until today. But—"

The rest of her words were smothered as his mouth crushed hers. It was a hot kiss, full of hunger and need. A need that Olivia knew was purely physical. Yet she couldn't seem to fight it, or him. Something in the taste of his lips, the feel of his strong hands on her back, urging her against him, blotted all common sense from her thoughts. Unwillingly, her mouth opened beneath his, her hands flattened against the warm flesh above his waistband.

Olivia didn't know how long the kiss lasted. It seemed like forever, yet not nearly long enough. She only knew she was breathless and shaking by the time he lifted his mouth from hers.

"So you haven't forgiven me?" he murmured thoughtfully, his eyes searching her upturned face. "I wonder how you would kiss me if you had?"

Olivia wondered herself. She'd always behaved wantonly where Sam was concerned. It was something she couldn't seem to control. Even now, after four years and thousands of miles between them, she still wanted him physically. It didn't make sense!

"I wouldn't hold my breath waiting to find out if I were you," she said in a brittle voice. "Because you've just managed to bring me to my senses."

Before Sam could make any sort of response, Olivia twisted away from him and flew up the stairs. Eventually he became aware that his fists were clenched at his sides, causing pain to shoot through his cut fingers.

Cursing softly, no longer hungry, he put away the food and headed across the breezeway to the den. Right now that brandy his mother had offered him earlier this evening sounded pretty good.

Chapter Four

It was still dark the next morning when Sam came downstairs. He felt sluggish and groggy from lack of sleep. Along with that, he felt very foolish. He'd planned on treating Olivia with cool indifference. Instead he'd ended up kissing her. Twice. Damn it all, there was no telling what she was thinking. Probably that he still wanted her, he thought grimly. But she'd be wrong about that. Sam didn't want or need any woman. Olivia had cured him of such things. She'd shown him what it was like to want, to need, to love. And then to have it all taken away.

Down in the kitchen, Sam found his mother and sister preparing breakfast.

"Where's Dad?" he asked as he headed to the coffeepot.

Ella smashed a patty of frying sausage with a metal spatula. "He's gone to feed the hogs," she said.

He took a careful sip from his coffee cup. "I always do that. He should have stayed in bed."

"Daddy stay in bed? You must be kidding," Kathleen said as she busily buttered bread for toast. "I really don't know if he'll be able to stand retirement. He certainly won't if he stays around here."

"Your father didn't want you doing anything with that cut hand." Ella waved the spatula at her son as she spoke. "As for S.T. being retired, I think he'll make it just fine once we move down by his brother, Jim. They'll have so much fishing and hunting to do together, he'll never realize he's not working."

S.T. had actually already retired from the farm, and as soon as the weather grew warm this spring, he planned to move to East Texas to be close to his brother. Sam would be taking over the farm completely. He liked the idea that his parents would finally be able to relax and enjoy themselves, and he liked the idea of managing the farm totally by himself.

From the time Sam had been big enough to ride with his father on a tractor, he'd known being a farmer was what he wanted. That had never changed for Sam. Not even when Olivia had tried her best to get him to leave it and go with her to Africa.

She'd never seemed to understand that the farm was his life. It represented who he was and what he was. His Gallagher ancestors had toiled the very same fields that Sam worked now. It had been handed down from generation to generation, and now the time for Sam to take the reins had arrived. He knew it would be a different place once his parents were gone. Except for himself, the house would be totally empty.

From the time Sam was old enough to think about such things, he'd pictured a wife and family in his life. When he'd met and fallen in love with Olivia that picture had become a real dream, one he'd planned to have come true. Olivia had been different from any other woman he'd known. She cared about people, not things. She cared about him! And he'd imagined them filling the farmhouse with children of their own.

Sam's dream had died a bitter death when Olivia had left the farm, and shortly after, the country. He'd told himself he no longer loved her, but even so, he couldn't imagine sharing that same life with another woman.

"I'm wondering if I should go wake Olivia?" Kathleen asked her mother as she shoved a pan of buttered bread under the broiler. "I know she'll want to eat breakfast."

At the mention of Olivia's name, Sam looked over at the two women. "She probably needs sleep more than she needs food," he said.

"Sam's right," Ella replied. "The poor girl was tired after her long drive yesterday. We should have never kept her up so late watching that movie."

Sam stared into his coffee cup as he told himself he should have never kept her downstairs, and he certainly shouldn't have kissed her. Now he couldn't get her out of his mind.

With a worried grimace on her face, Kathleen tossed her long dark hair over her shoulder. "Yes. And I should have mentioned that we need to be careful about not tiring her out." She looked at Sam, then back to her mother. "Did she tell either of you that she's been ill?"

Olivia had been ill? The question stunned Sam.

"No!" Ella answered. "Has she been?"

Kathleen nodded glumly. "That's why she left Africa. The doctors ordered her to because she needed more rest."

"Oh dear," Ella said with quiet concern. "Why didn't she say anything about it to us?"

"You know Olivia, she doesn't want a fuss made over her. So for heaven's sake don't mention it to her."

Sam stared at the two women, still unable to believe what he was hearing. Olivia had been sent home from Africa because of her health? Why hadn't she told him last night?

"Good morning. Am I too late for breakfast?"

All heads turned to see Olivia entering the kitchen. The first thing Sam noticed was that her blond hair was pulled back into a tight French braid. There were faint shadows of fatigue under her eyes, but they were hardly enough to detract from her beauty.

She was dressed in jeans and a black sweater with a reindeer appliquéd on the chest. She must have purchased winter clothing since she'd returned to the States, he thought. They were obviously new and of the latest fashion. Sam's eyes traveled over every petite curve as she moved into the kitchen.

"Oh, good morning, Olivia!" Kathleen exclaimed. "I— we were just talking about you."

Olivia smiled as she glanced around her, noticing the little things that most people took for granted. She'd almost forgotten what it was like to be around a family like the Gallaghers. To be in a farmhouse where everybody gathered in a big, warm kitchen for breakfast, with the smell of coffee and hickory-smoked bacon filling the air. Here Olivia could almost forget the dry African heat, the sickness, the starvation and the hopelessness.

"I hope it was all good," she said, forcing a cheery note to her voice.

"Uh, Kathleen and I were just saying that we wished you would marry," Ella put in. "Is there anyone back in Africa you have your heart set on?"

Sam had asked her the same question in a roundabout way, Olivia thought. She hadn't answered him. Mainly because she'd been too angry to do so. But Ella was truly sincere about Olivia's happiness, whereas Sam could hardly stand to be in the same room with her. Or so it seemed from the things he'd said to her last night.

"No, not really," Olivia answered honestly as she went to pour herself a cup of coffee. "There was someone for a while, but we decided we were better at being friends than we would be as lovers.''

Kathleen looked up curiously as she retrieved the toast from the oven. "Did you talk about marriage?"

Olivia was careful not to look in Sam's direction. "He proposed. But I couldn't accept."

Ella chuckled as she carried a plate of bacon and sausages over to the kitchen table. "Didn't make you swoon, eh?"

Swoon? The only man who'd ever made Olivia swoon was Sam Gallagher. As if they had a will of their own, her eyes slipped over to the object of her thoughts. He was standing by the row of windows that overlooked the river. His face was turned toward the view, making it impossible to guess what he was thinking. "I'm twenty-six years old, Ella," she said in a teasing voice. "I'm past the swooning age."

The older woman laughed. "Don't tell S.T. that. He thinks he can make me swoon any time of the day."

Olivia didn't doubt that. Even after raising three children, and years of hard work making the farm successful, Ella and S.T. had a close, affectionate relationship. It was obvious to anyone who looked that the two of them adored each other.

Olivia was envious of the invisible bond the older couple shared. She knew she would probably never experience that kind of love or companionship. Each time she had tried to think seriously about a man, Sam had always stood in the back of her mind, reminding her that love could wind up being a very painful thing.

Her gaze turned to the object of her thoughts. "How's your hand this morning, Sam?"

Slowly his head turned until he was looking directly at her. Faint surprise showed in his brown eyes, telling her he hadn't expected any sort of greeting from her this morning.

"It's stiff and sore. But it doesn't ache anymore."

She forced herself to smile at him. In spite of all he'd said and done, she could not hate him. Moreover, she didn't want him to hate her. She wanted them to at least be friends. "That's good. Maybe if you put a heavy leather glove on it before you go out, it will help protect it."

"Olivia's advice is well-meaning, Sam," Ella told her son. "But I'm going to go a step further and tell you there's not a thing you need to be doing today."

"I may not *need* to do anything," he corrected his mother, "but I might want to."

Kathleen glanced around at her brother. "Well, there was something I needed for you to help me with, but now that you've hurt your hand I suppose Olivia and I can manage," she said.

Olivia turned toward her friend. "Manage to do what?"

Kathleen handed Olivia a plate of toast to carry to the table while she gathered a jar of jam and a pot of honey.

As both women carried their load to the table, Kathleen said, "I have several cases of canned food to be taken into town. It's for the food drive that the troops at Fort Chaffee put on every year. They distribute the canned goods to needy people who would otherwise not have a Thanksgiving dinner. And since Thanksgiving is only two days away, I'd better get mine delivered."

Olivia set the plate of toast on the table, then glanced at Sam, who was still standing by the windows. Her expression dared him to make a cutting remark about her own job with the needy. However, for the moment she was surprised to see there was no mockery or cynicism on his face.

"I can still do it, Kathleen. I have one good hand. With you and Olivia helping, we should be able to get it all loaded."

Kathleen smiled gratefully at her brother. "Thanks, Sam. I knew I loved you for some reason."

He grinned impishly at his sister. It was the first glimpse Olivia had of the Sam she used to know, and the sight lifted her heart. Maybe the Sam she'd fallen in love with hadn't turned totally cynical. Maybe this Thanksgiving wasn't going to be as terrible as she'd first feared.

"I thought it was my charm and good looks," he teased.

The door to the kitchen opened and a gust of icy wind whirled past S.T.'s tall, burly figure. He stomped the mud from his boots and tugged off his gloves. "Breakfast ready, Ma?"

"You have the nose of a hound dog, S.T.," Ella said. On her way to the table she smacked a kiss on her husband's cheek. "Either that, or you were upwind of the hog pen."

S.T. laughed as he walked over to the kitchen sink and washed his hands. "I can smell your cooking anytime, anywhere, Elly girl."

Once he was finished, he went over and curled his arm around Olivia's shoulders. "Come on, Olivia," he said, guiding her toward the long oak table. "Let's get started. I'll bet you haven't had good homemade sausage since you left Arkansas."

For a second Olivia fondly snuggled her head against the crook of his shoulder. There had been lots of things Olivia hadn't had while she'd been abroad. But the thing she'd missed most of all was this family. Its warmth and love. Something Olivia had never had from her own family. Something she doubted she would ever find elsewhere.

Last night, when Sam had stung her with hateful words, she'd thought coming back had been a mistake. But now she was more determined than ever not to let Sam ruin her precious time here on the Gallagher farm.

After breakfast Olivia found herself in Sam's pickup truck, sandwiched between him and Kathleen. The morning was cold but bright as the three of them traveled northeast through Van Buren, then Alma. There, Sam turned onto Highway 71 which headed into the Boston Mountains.

Almost all of the bright foliage had already fallen from the trees, making Olivia wish she had driven up sooner to see the mountains in all their autumn splendor. But to be honest, the past few weeks since she'd been back from Africa, she hadn't had the inclination to do anything. She'd had to force herself to go out and buy new winter clothing. And she'd only done that out of necessity; in Ethiopia she'd needed only summer things.

"I suppose the fall colors were beautiful this year," she remarked, unaware of the wistful sound in her voice.

Hearing it, Sam cast her a thoughtful glance. Had she actually missed Arkansas? he wondered. Had she missed him? He doubted it. After their argument about her going to work in Africa, she'd left the farm angry, telling Sam she didn't care whether she ever saw or spoke to him again in her life. But six weeks later he'd received a letter posted from Addis Ababa, Ethiopia.

Sam hadn't opened it. Nor had he opened the others that had followed. He regretted that now. But at the time he'd been so angry and hurt that his male pride had cried out for retaliation. He'd written Return to Sender across the front and put them back in the mail. Now he wondered just exactly what she had written to him. And wondered, too, if it would have made a difference to their lives.

"We had plenty of rain this summer," Sam told her, "so the trees were especially pretty. I tried to get Kathleen to take a drive with me up to Eureka Springs, but she wouldn't go."

Puzzled, Olivia looked at her friend. "Why wouldn't you go, Kathleen? You love that place. All the quaint shops and winding streets."

Kathleen shrugged as she kept her face turned to the window. "I just... wasn't in the mood."

"Truth is, Olivia, Kathleen hadn't been in the mood for anything until she heard you were coming," Sam said.

"That's not true, brother! Why, for the past two weeks, I've been doing a lot. Like getting this food for the troop drive."

Olivia exchanged concerned glances with Sam, then said, "Kathleen, I don't want to hear that you've been feeling sorry for yourself."

Kathleen turned an indignant expression on her brother and her friend. "I haven't been feeling sorry for myself. I've just been . . . lost," she added quietly.

Olivia was feeling rather lost herself, but Kathleen didn't need to hear that. And she certainly didn't want Sam to know it. He'd probably just throw her defeat up in her face, and enjoy doing it.

Reaching over, Olivia squeezed Kathleen's fingers. "Well, before I leave Arkansas I'm going to make sure you're not lost anymore."

Kathleen mustered a smile. "What are you going to do? Hang a cowbell around my neck?"

"Hmm, that might be an idea," Sam teased. "I'll see if I can find one down at the barn."

Kathleen's house was a split-level, built on the side of a mountain. It was huge in size, the many windows lining the front framed by dark gray shutters. To the right, where the ground ran flat for a few hundred feet, was a small tennis court, and a swimming pool presently covered from the elements.

Olivia was surprised by the whole place. She'd expected something more homey and less showy. But then she'd never met Kathleen's late husband. This must have reflected his sort of life-style.

Sam backed the truck close to the garage door, where all three of them climbed down from the cab. While Kathleen went to open the door electronically, Olivia looked around her and tried to imagine her down-to-earth friend living here.

"I hope I haven't waited too late to get these things delivered," Kathleen said as the three of them entered the garage.

"My word, Kathleen! What were you trying to do? Buy the whole grocery store out?" Sam asked, amazed at the sight before him.

"You know I have more than enough to take care of my needs. And just think of how many children this will help on Thanksgiving."

Olivia was inclined to agree with Sam. Kathleen had gone a little bit overboard. Cases and cases of food were stacked nearly as high as Olivia's head. But she supposed the idea of helping others had, in turn, helped Kathleen. Sam must have thought so, too, because he didn't say anything else about the matter.

"You didn't stack all this food by yourself, did you?" Olivia asked Kathleen as the three of them started loading the cases onto the pickup bed.

"No. The grocery store was more than happy to deliver it for me. Of course I don't know about the poor kid who had to unload it."

From inside the house, a telephone rang. Hearing it, Kathleen hurried over to a door that entered into the house. "I need to answer that," she told them. "It might be the real estate agent I've been trying to get in touch with."

After a scramble with the lock, Kathleen flew into the house. When the ringing stopped and she didn't return immediately, Sam sat down on the open tailgate of the truck.

"We might as well take a break while she's on the phone," he suggested.

Olivia jammed her mittened hands into her coat pockets. "I don't know if I want to quit working or not. I might freeze to death if I stop moving."

"Freeze! Why, it's probably forty-five degrees," he said.

Olivia didn't know whether he was serious or merely making fun of her. She jumped up on the other end of the tailgate and turned her collar up around her neck. "I'm more used to ninety-five degrees. This is the first time I've had a coat on in years."

Olivia's admission had Sam's gaze turning her way. The cold wind had flushed her cheeks and nose a bright pink and torn wisps of hair loose from her braid. She looked much younger than her twenty-six years. There was still a tender, innocent quality about her face, and that surprised him. He'd expected her to come back hardened. But then Sam was only looking at the outside. Who knew what she was like on the inside? He'd once thought he did, but he'd been fooled.

"Your being here is good for Kathleen," he said. "She's been a different person ever since she heard you were coming."

Olivia was surprised to hear him admit that her coming to his home was not a complete mistake. But then she knew how much Sam loved his sister. He could put up with anyone for a few days if he thought it might help Kathleen.

"I was stunned when I got her letter about her husband's accident," Olivia told him. "I called her immediately after I read it. I wanted badly to comfort her, but I didn't really know what to say. In fact, Kathleen didn't talk about him or what had happened. Instead, she asked all about me and acted as though she were fine. I could hear the pain in her voice, though."

Sam nodded, then sighed heavily as he looked across the mountainside. "I wish she'd go back to teaching. She needs something in her life."

"We all need something," Olivia said ruefully, thinking about her own uncertain future. "The question is finding it."

His brown eyes cut an accusing path to her face. "You didn't have any trouble finding it. I guess as long as you have a hungry mouth to feed, you'll have all you ever need."

There was no sarcasm in his voice, yet the flat certainty with which he spoke cut into her. Sam didn't know her. He didn't know how alone she often felt. He didn't know of the many nights she cried herself to sleep. Not just for the babies she saw literally dying before her eyes, but also for that empty place inside her that nothing ever seemed to fill.

Her parents distanced themselves from her. The only man she'd ever loved was estranged from her. All she had was her work. Sam thought that was all she wanted or needed. But now she didn't even have that. The irony of it burned her throat with tears.

"Well," she said, her voice low, "it's a cinch the world will never be free of hungry people. Things are getting worse rather than better."

As he watched her, he wondered again about the illness that had supposedly sent her back here to the States. She didn't appear sickly, but he could sense a despondency about her that she hadn't had four years ago.

"I thought by now you'd know that the world will never be free from hunger or poverty."

Her blue eyes were shadowed with disappointment as she studied his face. "You sound like a cynic, Sam. Where is that coming from? I remember a time when you talked of farming, and how good it made you feel to know that your job helped feed our nation."

Didn't Olivia realize that he didn't want to think about those times they'd walked through the fields hand in hand, talking quietly, sometimes laughing? In those days the sun had warmed their faces and their love for each other had warmed their hearts. At least, Sam had believed it was love on his part.

Looking away from her, he fastened his gaze on the toe of his boot. "It still makes me feel good, Olivia, to know that my crops are helping to feed people here at home, and even some abroad. But I'm not foolish enough to think I alone can save the world from starvation."

The way she had? The words hung between them even if he hadn't spoken them. And maybe that had been her problem, she thought sadly. Maybe she'd gone to Africa with her expectations too high. But how could it be foolish to want to save all the starving, instead of only some of them?

Sliding down from her seat on the tailgate, she stood in front of him, her expression challenging. "The Sam Gallagher I knew cared about people. He always put everyone else's needs before himself. What happened to that man?"

Sam shoved himself off the tailgate to stand only inches away from Olivia. The closeness forced her to bend her head back in order to see his face. As she looked up at him, she felt a quiver rush through her that had nothing to do with the cold wind.

"I still care about people, Olivia, and I try to help them whenever it's possible. But that doesn't mean I'm supposed to take on everyone else's problems. A man's first responsibility is to his family."

And Olivia wasn't part of his family. He couldn't have put it more clearly if he'd tried. She felt her heart begin to tear, and the pain of it showed in her blue eyes. "Do you know what it did to me, Sam, when you said you wouldn't marry me and go with me to Africa?"

Sam stared down at Olivia, so stunned by her question that he could say nothing. What was she trying to tell him? And why did she look so wounded? He was the one who'd been left behind.

"Of course I know what it did," he replied bitingly. "It made you see that your plan to pull me into your self-righteous ideals wasn't going to work. And that made you angry."

Her head jerked from side to side. "My God, Sam!"

She wanted to say more. She tried to say more, but she was too hurt to speak. Tense moments passed as their eyes clashed, his full of defiance, hers dark with angry disbelief.

From somewhere inside her, she eventually found the strength to turn her back to him. Instantly Sam caught hold of her, and Olivia could feel the iron bands of his fingers through the thickness of her coat.

"My God, what?" he muttered. "Why don't you finish? Because you know what I said was true? You went to Africa because you wanted to show your parents that you could live as opposite of their rich life-style as you could get. That meant more to you than staying here on the farm and being my wife!"

Pain and bitterness welled up in her throat. She tried her best to laugh it away. "There's no use in answering, Sam. You've got it all figured out."

With a phony smile plastered across her face, she twisted around to face him once again. "Besides," she said, her voice suddenly light and sweet, "none of that really matters now, does it? You have your life and I have mine. You and I are nothing more than old acquaintances crossing paths again. Don't you agree?"

Sam's hands tightened on her arms. His eyes sparked with the urge to jerk her into his arms and kiss the indifferent look off her face.

"I guess it must have been easy for you to go to Africa and forget a simple farm boy like me," he said, his voice dripping with sarcasm. "Wasn't it?"

Olivia looked into his brown eyes and felt something twist in her heart. Four years ago she'd believed her work was the most important thing in her life. And after Sam had refused to leave the farm and go with her to Africa, she'd thought she could forget him just as easily as he was saying she had. But it hadn't worked that way. Nothing had been easy for her since she'd walked away from this place.

"No, it wasn't easy, Sam. My letters would have proved that. If you'd just cared enough to read them."

Sam opened his mouth to ask her what a letter could have said that she couldn't have told him beforehand, but the sound of a door opening and shutting had him dropping his hands and turning away from her.

"Sorry I was gone so long," Kathleen said as she joined them at the truck. She looked quizzically from Olivia's pinched expression to Sam's back. "That was Mom on the phone. She wants me to pick up some things at the mall. You don't mind driving by there, do you, Sam?"

Taking a deep, cleansing breath, Sam turned to face his sister. It was nearly Thanksgiving, he told himself, a time that had always been special for his family. He didn't want to allow thoughts of Olivia to weigh him down until he ruined the holiday for himself and everyone else.

"No, I don't mind," he said with a brief smile for his sister. "Now let's get the rest of this food loaded."

Sam headed into the garage. Behind him, Kathleen took hold of Olivia's arm. "Are you all right?"

Olivia did her best to give her friend an innocent smile. "Of course I am. Why?"

Kathleen shrugged as her eyes continued to study Olivia's face. "You...just looked so pale when I came out. And Sam had such a glower on his face. What in the world was he saying to you?"

He was saying that he hated me, Olivia silently cried. She blinked her eyes furiously, hoping that if there were tears in them, Olivia would think it was only the effects of the cold wind. "Nothing much, just asking me about my work."

Kathleen didn't look too convinced, but since Sam was already approaching them with a load of canned goods in his arms, she let the matter drop.

After depositing the load of food at a nearby center, Sam drove them to the shopping mall and parked near the front entrance.

"If you two would rather sit and wait," Kathleen said, "it probably won't take me longer than fifteen minutes to pick up the things Mother has on her list."

Without looking at either woman, Sam said, "That's fine. But I'm sure Olivia would rather go with you, Kathleen. I'm going over to the hardware store to check on some fencing material."

Olivia glanced at his stern profile. She'd already suspected that the less time Sam spent in her presence, the better he'd like it, and he'd just proved her right. Sam didn't want her company anymore than she wanted his.

Olivia quickly turned to Kathleen, who was already climbing out the door of the pickup. "I think—"

Before she could say more, Kathleen was waving her hand in a dismissive way. "I'm going to have to walk from one end of the mall to the other. There's no need for Olivia to traipse after me. Besides, Sam, you and Olivia have hardly gotten to visit with each other."

Olivia knew she was caught as she glanced from sister to brother. What could she say without making it look like she was choosing one's company over the other? And why wasn't Sam saying anything? she wondered.

"I'll meet you back here in fifteen to twenty minutes," Kathleen went on before Olivia had the chance to object. "And if I'm not here, Sam, don't leave me to call a taxi."

He peered at Kathleen from beneath arched brows. "Since when have I ever left my sister behind?"

Kathleen merely laughed at the imperious sound of his voice. "You never have—yet, that is. But there's always a first time. When you get your mind on farming supplies, you're liable to forget.''

He snorted and turned the key in the ignition. It was a cinch his mind wasn't going to be on farming supplies. Not with Olivia going.

''We'll be here, and we'll wait,'' he said, trying to sound patient but doing a miserable job of it.

''Good, because I thought we could all have coffee somewhere before we went home,'' Kathleen said. She pulled the strap of her purse over her shoulder and winked at Olivia.

Sam began to curse. ''Damn it, Kathleen. I know it's nearly a holiday, but I have work waiting for me at the farm.''

Kathleen merely laughed. ''Well, that's nothing new for you, Sam. But Olivia and I have been working out in the cold. If you can't at least buy us a cup of coffee, Olivia is going to think you're a wretch.''

With that she shut the door and headed across the parking lot toward the massive building.

Sam pulled the truck into gear and gunned it out of the parking slot. He wanted to be annoyed with his sister, but he couldn't be. Not when he saw that she was showing more life than she had in a long time. Olivia might be tearing his own emotions apart, he thought, but she was certainly helping his sister's.

Olivia glanced over at his stern profile. Had he really become a wretch, as Kathleen had just implied? He'd hinted that her leaving had hurt him, but could it have really affected him that much? No. It couldn't have, she argued with herself. He hadn't loved her. Not really. Her leaving couldn't have changed him.

But Sam was different, she thought. So different from the man who'd given her all those quiet, sexy smiles, his brown eyes full of tender promises.

Beside him, Sam could feel Olivia's eyes quietly studying him. He wondered what she was thinking. He didn't understand her actions any more than he understood her words. Earlier at Kathleen's, she'd said so many things that had taken him by surprise. She'd kept implying that four years ago she had loved him. If that was really the case then why had she left? He realized a part of him would never rest until he knew what had really been in her heart.

"Well," Sam spoke as he pulled onto an adjacent street. "We can't have you thinking I'm a wretch. So I guess I'll spring for coffee before we go home."

"I'm sure that will please Kathleen," Olivia said as casually as she could.

He didn't reply, but then he didn't have to, Olivia decided as she watched a tight grimace cross his face.

Sam glanced away from the busy traffic long enough to look at her. "What about you, Olivia? Will it please you, too?"

Chapter Five

Olivia was so surprised by his question that for long moments she could only stare at Sam. Why was he even bothering to ask her such a thing? she wondered. It was more than obvious that he didn't give a hoot whether anything he did pleased her.

She shrugged, determined to treat his question casually. "I'm game for anything. But don't put yourself out on my account. I'm just along for the ride."

A ride she obviously didn't want to be on, Sam thought. She shifted in the seat and crossed her legs. From the corner of his eye, Sam allowed his gaze to travel over the curve of her thigh and wondered why such a simple thing should affect him. He didn't want to be physically attracted to her and it shocked him because he was. They hadn't seen each other for four long years. He'd believed all those feelings had died with the passing time.

Impulsively, he flipped on the turn signal at the next intersection and turned right onto a busy thoroughfare. They traveled several blocks before he said, "You didn't really want to go to a hardware store, did you?"

Olivia had been gazing out the window, trying to forget that Sam was only a few inches away, but now she turned to look at him. "Is this a trick question?"

He responded with something between a snort and a laugh. "It's just a simple question, Olivia. Not a test."

A quizzical frown tugged at her features as she studied his profile. "Like I said before, I'm just a passenger. Don't worry about me. Besides, I can always wait in the truck while you look at fencing in the hardware store."

Olivia had never been a demanding person. Sam could see that hadn't changed about her. In fact, one of the things he remembered most was the way she'd always put everyone's wishes and wants before her own. That is, until it came to the matter of her going to Africa. Then there'd been no compromise.

"We're not going to the hardware store," he said bluntly.

Olivia's eyes widened at this bit of news. "Oh. Then where are we going?"

He inclined his head toward the next intersection. "Right up here."

Right up here turned out to be Creekmore Park. Olivia was surprised, to say the least. As he parked the truck, her mind searched for the motive that had prompted him to bring her to this city park.

"Would you like to get out and walk some of the footpaths? We have at least ten more minutes or so to kill," he said as he twisted the key and cut the truck engine.

Awkward silence filled the cab, making Olivia even more aware of his presence. She glanced at him, then hastily began buttoning her coat. There was no way she could stay confined this closely to Sam for ten minutes and keep her sanity, she decided.

"Sure," she told him. "But what about your fencing material?"

He shook his head. "I have enough to start with back at the farm. I was just…more or less wanting to check prices." And deter her from coming with him, Sam thought. But since that hadn't worked, he'd found himself driving here instead.

"I see," Olivia said.

The brief smile on her face was nothing more than a movement of her lips, telling Sam that she really did see beneath his words. And that bothered him. For reasons he wasn't quite ready to examine.

The two of them left the truck and began walking down one of the paths that led through towering hardwood trees. Even though the sun was now shining brightly, the day was still cool to Olivia. As they walked, she pulled on a pair of red mittens to protect her hands against the cold wind.

"I don't suppose you saw trees like this over in Ethiopia," Sam said after they'd walked a few yards.

"No," she told him. "And you can't imagine how nice it is to be out like this now." She took a deep breath and tilted her head back in order to see the branches entwined far above their heads. Most of the leaves had fallen, but here and there splashes of red and gold still clung tenaciously against the onslaught of winter. "Until I went to Africa I didn't appreciate just how beautiful Arkansas trees were in autumn."

Sam looked at Olivia and wondered if four years ago he had appreciated just how beautiful she was. One thing for sure, he was certainly appreciating it now. As he took in the sparkle in her eyes, the soft smile on her face, he realized this woman beside him was more than just beautiful.

Her beauty didn't come from the shape of her face, Sam decided. It wasn't the color of her hair, or the smoothness of her skin. It came from an inner warmth that radiated from her smile, her touch, her voice. It was something he'd never found in any other woman. Something that still drew him to her in spite of the past.

"Well, I think it's human nature to appreciate a thing more once we no longer have it," he said, his expression thoughtful as he looked away from her and out across the open woods of the park.

"Yes. You're probably right," she replied, the smile fading from her face. It was true, she thought. There had been many things in her life she'd taken for granted, many things she hadn't appreciated until they were missing. Sam most of all. But she doubted he would believe that, even if she tried to tell him.

Suddenly laughter sounded somewhere behind them, pushing the glum thought from Olivia's head. She and Sam both glanced over their shoulders, to see a young couple enjoying themselves as they attempted to walk a pair of frisky puppies.

"Oh, how cute!" Olivia exclaimed, watching the half-grown pups run circles around each other and the legs of their masters.

As the two of them watched the antics of the playful pups, Sam's hand unconsciously came up to rest against the small of Olivia's back. She was instantly aware of his touch and the warm thrill it sent coursing through her.

"Which pup do you like better?" Sam asked, his voice softening at the glow of pleasure on her face.

"Now that is a hard question," she said as she turned a smile on him. "I have to admit I love the dalmatian, but the collie is so pretty. It's going to grow up to look just like Lassie."

"I guess you haven't met Jake and Leo yet."

Olivia's brows lifted in question as she found herself looking straight into his face. At the moment his brown eyes were quiet and warm as they looked into hers. Even so, they still had the power to make her heart skip a beat.

"Who are Jake and Leo?" she asked, her eyes dropping to his lips, even though she told them not to.

"My two collies. They usually stay at the barn. That's probably why you haven't seen them around."

"Are they as smart as the Lassie on TV was?"

He grinned, making the lines around his eyes crinkle and his teeth flash against his dark skin. "Well, so far they haven't pulled anyone from a pit of quicksand, or dragged someone from a burning barn. But give them the opportunity and I'm sure they'd come through."

Olivia had to laugh. "I already feel safer just knowing they're on the farm."

In silent agreement, they began strolling up the walkway. After a few moments Sam realized his arm was at her waist. He didn't know when he'd actually put it there, but even more surprising was the realization that he didn't want to take it away. He wanted to keep touching her. He wanted to pretend for these few moments that she'd never gone to Africa, that for the past four years she'd spent her life with him.

"Last week I found a stray kitten outside my apartment," Olivia said, breaking the silence. "He was so cold and hungry I was tempted to keep him, but I ended up feeding him, then taking him to a humane shelter. Maybe some child will get him for Christmas."

Sam wondered if she realized how wistful she sounded. "Why didn't you keep it?" he asked. "If I remember right, you used to love animals."

"I still do."

"Then why..." he paused and glanced her way. "Oh, I wasn't thinking. I guess it would be a problem taking a pet back to Africa with you."

Olivia had almost forgotten that Sam believed she was returning to Africa. A part of her wanted to tell him that she'd decided to quit her relief work. But she stopped herself. Just because he'd shown her a few minutes of civility didn't mean he felt any differently toward her. If he knew she had failed at her work, he would probably take great pleasure in rubbing it in her face. More than likely he'd even laugh and say I told you so. Olivia couldn't take that from him. Not now.

Not trusting herself to look at him, she murmured, "Yes, it would be a problem to ship a pet that far. Maybe I should have given him to Kathleen. She always loved cats."

His mouth twisted ruefully. "Yeah, she did. Until Greg made her get rid of her pets."

"Oh? He didn't like animals?"

He muttered an oath just under his breath. "Greg liked himself. He sure didn't want cat hair on his tailored suits."

It was obvious from the sound of Sam's voice that he didn't think too highly of Kathleen's late husband. Olivia knew Greg had been a businessman, but she also knew that Sam would never hold that against anyone. "I can't imagine Kathleen living with a man like that."

"Well, she doesn't anymore."

"No. She doesn't," Olivia echoed with a trace of sadness.

"Speaking of my sister, we'd better head back to the mall. She might be waiting for us," Sam said.

Olivia nodded in agreement and they turned back. Even though it was a weekday, there were several people in the park—mothers and children, joggers and walkers. As they drew nearer to where Sam had parked the truck, two young women jogged past. Olivia couldn't help but notice their interest in Sam.

To know that he attracted other women didn't surprise her. But she suspected it would have surprised Sam. He seemed unconscious of his own good looks and perhaps that guilelessness made him even more attractive. Today his long lean body was covered with jeans, a brown cotton shirt and a denim jacket. His black hair was too straight and strong to stay put in one place. Most of it had now fallen over his forehead, even though he pushed it back from time to time with an impatient hand. The black stubble that had been on his face last night when he'd kissed her was even longer now, giving him a dark, roguish look.

That kiss, she thought, sighing inwardly. She shouldn't be thinking about it now. She shouldn't be thinking about it at all. There could never be anything between her and Sam. He'd only kissed her to punish her. So why couldn't she forget it?

The two of them traveled the few miles back to the shopping mall in silence. When Sam parked the truck near the front entrance, Kathleen was nowhere in sight.

"Kathleen has obviously forgotten the time," he said, switching off the ignition key. "She probably found a sale she couldn't resist."

"Please don't get angry with her," Olivia said, remembering his earlier warning to his sister.

Amused at her concern, he chuckled softly. "I never get angry with Kathleen. I only pretend to be. She knows that."

He might only pretend to be angry with his sister, but he certainly hadn't been pretending last night with her, Olivia thought grimly. But that was something she couldn't keep dwelling on. She was going to be in this man's house for the next few days and she couldn't survive that time if she allowed the past to take over.

"So. How have your crops done this past year?" she asked, shifting in the seat so that she was facing him.

Sam had to bite his tongue to keep from reminding her that the farm had never interested her in the past. But he didn't want to have an argument with her. Especially when Kathleen would be showing up at any minute.

"This past harvest was good. The year before was not so good. Oklahoma was flooded with spring rains, which eventually caused the Arkansas to go over its banks. A major part of our fields were covered with at least five or six feet of water."

Olivia could only imagine what the flooding had done, not only to the fields, but also to the farm's finances. "Had you already planted?"

Sam nodded. "It was hell trying to get the fields back into shape to plant again. By the time I did, it was too late for a spring spinach crop."

Until Olivia had met Kathleen, farming had been something totally unfamiliar to her. From her few visits to the Gallagher farm, she'd seen the hard work that went into it. But it hadn't been until she went to Africa that she actually realized just how important farming was to a country. "How long does your father plan to continue working? I thought he'd be retired by now."

As she spoke, Sam's gaze wandered over her face, silently admiring the delicate rise of her cheekbones, the sweep of thick lashes veiling her eyes, the curve of her soft lips. The image of her face had never faded from his mind. He'd told himself it had. But yesterday when he'd seen her for the first time in four years, he knew with startling clarity that he hadn't forgotten a thing about her.

"You might as well say he's retired now. This year he mostly puttered around the barn and enjoyed taking care of the hogs."

In spite of the busy parking lot with people and traffic moving to and fro, Olivia was acutely aware of the man beside her. His thigh was only inches away from hers, his shoulder almost close enough to brush against hers. He smelled of woods and wild grasses, the same sensuous scent that had swirled around her last night when he'd taken her in his arms. She could feel his eyes upon her, drawing her to him like an unspoken word.

Hoping to push the intimate thoughts aside, she forced herself to speak. "So... how does it feel to be in charge of things?"

One corner of his mouth curved into a faint smile. "It feels good. I like being the boss."

No doubt, she thought wryly. Didn't all men like being the boss? Or was it just strong-minded, self-assured men like Sam? "But you only have yourself to boss. If you make mistakes now, they're all yours."

"I'm not afraid to make mistakes. I've made them before."

Did he mean he'd made a mistake with her? Or maybe he considered it a mistake to have ever gotten involved with her in the first place? The questions were in her eyes long before she could put them into words.

She was opening her mouth to speak when the truck door opened beside her and cold air wooshed into the warm confines of the cab.

A little out of breath, Kathleen began to hurriedly explain, "Sorry I'm late. I just happened to see some jewelry on sale and I couldn't resist going through it."

Sam flicked Olivia a pointed look that said I told you so. She couldn't help but smile back at him, while thinking that he certainly knew his sister. Too bad he'd never known *her* that well, she thought a little sadly.

Kathleen climbed into the cab, forcing Olivia to slide over to the middle of the seat. She did her best to keep a small space between her and Sam, but by the time Kathleen made room for herself and her packages, Olivia was jammed up against Sam.

As he leaned forward to start the truck, Olivia tried not to think about his shoulder brushing against hers, or the way her thigh was pressed against the long length of his. Touching him, even out of necessity, sent a trembling warmth rushing through her.

While Sam backed out of the parking slot, she took a deep breath and prayed that the trip home would be short and that neither Sam nor Kathleen would notice the telltale color on her cheeks.

"Here," Kathleen said, handing her a package. "You'd better hold the pie plates. If they were to get broken, Mother would have a fit and send us straight back here for more."

Olivia took the package and settled it safely on her lap. "I can't see Ella having a fit over anything. She's too nice for that."

Sam laughed. "Then you don't know our mother. When she goes on the warpath even the dogs run and hide."

Olivia was beginning to think she didn't know Sam, either. At least, she'd never thought him capable of harboring such bitterness and cynicism as he'd shown her yesterday and last night. But then, she'd never dreamed that anything about him would still affect her. And as the movement of Sam's leg caused it to press more closely to hers, Olivia realized she'd never been more wrong.

It was almost lunchtime when the three of them arrived at the farm. Ella was in the kitchen rolling out pie dough and waiting impatiently for the pie plates to put it in.

"We could have been back here an hour ago, but Kathleen wanted to have coffee," Sam told his mother. "Just as though there wasn't any coffee here at home to drink."

Kathleen laughed, obviously knowing her brother's dry sarcasm was his way of teasing her. Olivia watched her give his arm an affectionate tug, and wondered what it would be like if she could be that close to him.

"Mother, you know how festive the mall is during the holidays. I just wanted to drink a little of it in and get into the spirit. Unlike Sam Scrooge here," she said of her brother. "Besides, I found some great jewelry. And Olivia, I bought you a pair of earrings that are going to go great with that amber-colored dress you showed me last night."

The women gathered around Kathleen as she emptied her purchases onto the kitchen table. While they were occupied with the jewelry, Sam reached for his work coat and went out the door.

He'd lost a lot of work time this morning, he told himself as he headed to the barn. It was time to get back to business, and definitely time to get himself away from Olivia. Earlier, in the park, he'd felt a part of him softening toward her, and he cursed himself for being so foolish and weak where she was concerned. She would hurt him again if he'd let her. But Sam was determined that this time with Olivia was going to be different.

He'd been working under the tractor for more than an hour when he heard footsteps. Sam figured they belonged to his father, but when he craned his neck in order to see, he discovered a pair of black suede flats and shapely legs encased in blue denim near his head.

With slow, deliberate movements he put the crescent wrench he'd been using to one side and wriggled his way from beneath the belly of the tractor.

Olivia's mouth went suddenly dry as Sam rose to his feet and stood before her. Grease was smeared along one rigid jaw, and his brown eyes pierced her from beneath the fall of black hair on his forehead.

His bandaged hand was growing stiff from the cold and limited movement. He tried flexing it and winced inwardly at the pain shooting through his fingers. "What are you doing down here? Isn't a barn a little out of your league?"

So, he was back to digging at her, she thought sadly. This morning at the park she'd almost believed he was going to put his bitterness aside. She should have known better. "I don't really think you know what kind of places I'm used to, Sam," she said.

Even though her voice was calm, there was a faint hint of challenge in the way her chin tilted. She was beautiful; Sam couldn't deny it. No more than he could deny that his heart had lifted the moment he'd seen it was her instead of his father standing beside the tractor.

"Maybe I don't. So what kind of places are you comfortable in, Miss Olivia Wescott?"

She handed him the brown paper bag she was holding in her hands, then walked over to what she figured was some sort of harvesting machine. It was massive and would take a bit of climbing just for her to reach the cab.

"You missed lunch. Your mother wanted me to bring you a couple of sandwiches. They're roast beef, I think. There's a thermos of coffee with them," she told him.

Not bothering to look inside the sack she'd given him, Sam walked toward her. "You didn't answer my question."

No, how could she? Olivia asked herself. She didn't know where she belonged anymore. She'd thought she belonged in Africa. She'd thought her desire to save others had meant more than anything. She'd been wrong. And because of it, Sam now hated her.

The thought was so painful she tried not to think about it as she turned to face him. "You know, Sam, you've always known where you belonged. Not all people are that lucky. Some people wander through their lives trying to figure out what they were really meant to do or be. I guess you've always known."

An old hay baler was parked just to the right of him. Sam set the sack of lunch on its fender as he pondered her pensive words. "I guess I have," he told her.

Olivia glanced back up at the piece of machinery behind her. "You don't ever have doubts? Or wonder if maybe you were supposed to have done something else with your life?"

He shook his head. "A Gallagher has been working this farm for more than a hundred years. As soon as I was old enough to know what that meant, I knew I wanted to do the same thing."

She sighed as she tried to imagine that sort of family pride and tradition. "The reconstruction period after the Civil War was a difficult time. I wonder how your ancestors ever made a go of this place."

"Irish determination, I suppose," he said with a wry twist to his mouth.

"And maybe a little Irish stubbornness to go along with it," she added on a teasing note.

He chuckled, but Olivia could hear a wealth of pride in his voice. "Probably some of that, too."

"My father couldn't have cared less about his ancestors," she admitted, wondering what it would be like to have a close-knit family, full of pride and love for each other. "He considered them all losers. Maybe that was because they didn't leave anything behind for him."

She leaned against a tire that was far taller than her head. "My parents are material people. I guess I told you that before. A long time ago—" She broke off to glance at him. He was only a step away from her now. So close but still so far, she thought.

"Yes. You told me," he said, wondering why the lost, pained look on her face should touch him so.

"That's why I've tried so hard not to be." She shook her head, then, closing her eyes, drew in a long, shaky breath. "I guess you were right about that, Sam. I guess I went to extreme lengths not to be like my parents."

His brown eyes narrowed, then darkened as he watched her. What was she saying? Reaching out, he closed his fingers around her chin and the side of her face. "Four years later is a hell of a time to be realizing that!"

Her eyes flew open, and she found his face only inches from hers. In spite of the cold temperature in the barn, his fingers were warm against her skin. She could feel the grainy texture of dirt and grease and knew that he was marking her face, but she didn't care. From the time she'd left this farm, she'd craved his touch. And now that she was back and so close to him once again, she realized she craved it even more.

"Yes, a hell of a time," she agreed.

Her whispered words not only touched him, they seeped inside him to some place he'd thought long dead.

Olivia felt his fingers tighten on her cheek, watched his mouth draw near to hers.

"This morning you asked me if I knew what it did to you when we parted. Well, I'm wondering if you've ever thought what it did to me. Did you think I was heartless? That I was just a plowboy you could carelessly fling aside while you went on your merry way?"

Olivia no longer had to wonder whether her leaving had really hurt him. She could see the pain in his brown eyes, feel it in the quiver of his fingers, hear it throbbing through his voice. God, what had she done to him? What had she done to herself?

"Sam—" Her throat closed around his name as her hands latched onto the front of his jacket. "I—I never meant to hurt you. Can't you understa—"

"Damn it! You're hurting me now! Do you understand that?"

Olivia didn't have a chance to even think about answering. His lips swooped down on hers like a hungry hawk savaging its prey.

Her fingers clung tightly to his jacket as desire numbed her mind and flooded her limbs with weakness. No matter if he hated her, no matter if he wanted to punish her. She wanted him, wanted the sweet, dark mystery of his mouth, wanted his arms around her, cocooning her in his strength and his warmth.

Olivia's heated response broke through his frustration. He could feel her lips straining against his, could feel her hands creep up the front of his jacket, then curve against the back of his head.

He didn't understand her response any more than he understood his own desire. He only knew that the more he touched her, the more he wanted her. And right now he wanted her with a vengeance.

"Sam, I... Please don't hate me," she whispered haltingly as his lips left hers to slide along the tender column of her throat.

Hate her? Did she think this was hating her? Had she gone crazy, or had he? He couldn't think. He didn't want to think. She had moved her hands from his neck and had snaked them under the edges of his jacket to slide up his back. The movement drew their bodies closer, making Sam groan as her hips wantonly pressed into his.

She was seducing him, turning his mind to useless pulp, he thought as he tasted the honey-soft skin of her neck, her chin, her cheeks. Another moment and she'd have him lowering her to the floor, making love to her, forgiving her for all the hurt she'd ever caused him.

Sam couldn't let her do that to him. Not again. He couldn't take what she was offering, then watch her leave again. It would kill him.

Calling on every ounce of willpower he possessed, he thrust her away from him. "I wish I could hate you, Olivia," he said, his voice ragged and accusing. "Then maybe I wouldn't want you like this, or any other damn way!"

Olivia could only stare at him. One minute she'd felt him kissing her, drawing her to him and now—now he was looking at her with venom in his eyes. "I thought..." She shook her head as tears began to form in her eyes. "It doesn't matter...."

Nothing mattered except getting out of the barn and away from his hard, accusing face. She turned away from him and began to run blindly through the maze of farming equipment.

The barn door was latched with a piece of heavy board. She was struggling to push it up and out of its notch when she heard Sam's footsteps behind her. Desperately she gave it one last shove and the door swung wide.

He called her name just as she ran out into the afternoon sunshine, but Olivia didn't stop. She wasn't going to turn back and give him the chance to cut her completely to shreds.

By the time she reached the house she'd managed to compose herself somewhat. Thankfully, when she entered the kitchen Kathleen was on the telephone, and Olivia could hear Ella in the utility room starting the washing machine. Without disturbing either of them, she hurried across the breezeway and up the stairs to her bedroom.

Moments later, when Kathleen entered her bedroom, Olivia was in the bathroom pressing a cold cloth to her eyes.

"Olivia, where are you?"

Olivia took a deep breath and pressed the cloth tighter. "In here, Kathleen. In the bathroom."

Her voice sounded normal enough. Maybe Kathleen wouldn't be able to see how much Sam had upset her.

The other woman leaned against the doorjamb and studied Olivia's image in the vanity mirror. "What are you doing? You flew through the kitchen like the devil was on your tail!"

That's because he had been, Olivia thought grimly.

"I, uh, I got something in my eye down at the barn and I've been trying to wash it out."

"Oh. Let me see," Kathleen said, quickly shoving herself away from the doorjamb and into the room. "Maybe I can get it."

Seeing she had no other choice, Olivia lowered the washcloth and blinked her bleary red eyes at her friend.

However, Kathleen barely glanced at her eyes. Instead she was studying the black, greasy fingerprints on Olivia's cheek and chin. "What's this?"

Olivia could feel red heat flooding her cheeks. "It's... grease. Sam, uh, put it there when—when he was looking in my eye."

Kathleen stepped back from Olivia and gave her a long, knowing look. "Yeah. And my name is Mr. Magoo."

With a flustered hand, Olivia began to wipe haphazardly at the grease Sam had left on her face. "You act as though you don't believe me."

"I don't."

Olivia heaved out a long breath and continued to wash her face.

"So what did my brother do to make you cry? I know you have been. So don't try denying it."

Olivia looked into the vanity mirror instead of at Kathleen. "You wouldn't understand if I told you. Just put it down to the fact that he's an ass! A complete, utter ass!"

She tossed the washcloth back into the sink, then raked a hand through her tousled blond hair. Kathleen began to laugh.

"You love him. Don't you?"

Stunned, Olivia turned to look at her friend. "Why do you say that?"

Kathleen smiled and shrugged. "Because a woman doesn't get this emotional over a man unless she loves him."

Knowing it would be futile to deny it, Olivia's head swung glumly from side to side. "I've cared about Sam for a long time, Kathleen. Ever since I spent those three weeks here on the farm with you after our college graduation.''

Kathleen's brows inched upward. "Olivia! That's years ago! Are you telling me that you and Sam were...that you cared about my brother before you left for Africa?"

Olivia nodded miserably. "I don't think I really knew just how much I cared for him until I left. But by then things had— Well, he didn't want me to leave. He couldn't understand my need to go to Africa—and because I did, he hates me.''

It was obvious Kathleen didn't know what to think. She eased away from the door and went to sit on the end of the bed.

Olivia followed, loosening her disheveled braid as she went. Her eyes were full of regret as she faced her friend. "I guess you're angry with me, too. Now that you know."

Kathleen's thoughtful expression turned to one of dismay. "Angry with you? Why should I be angry?"

Olivia's hand waved the air with a helpless gesture. "Because I hurt your brother, I suppose."

Kathleen grimaced. "From the look of things he hurt you just as badly. Now I understand why there's so much tension in the air when you two are around each other."

Sighing, Olivia walked over to the window and drew the yellow priscilla aside. From this view she could see several barns and storage buildings. In the distance was open, plowed ground, then a glimpse of the Arkansas River. This wasn't just a place that Sam lived or worked. It was a very part of him. Olivia could see that now. And she could see that she'd been foolish to think she could ever separate him from it.

"I was crazy to accept your mother's invitation. I should have known Sam wouldn't want me here." Her voice began to wobble as she dropped the curtain and turned to Kathleen. "But I wanted to see you and your parents again. I guess deep down I even wanted to see Sam again. Although I told myself I didn't.''

"If you hadn't agreed to spend Thanksgiving with us, I'd have driven to Little Rock and dragged you here," Kathleen insisted.

Her expression wistful, Olivia pushed both hands through her fine blond hair. "Now I'm going to ruin your holiday."

Kathleen rose from the bed and took Olivia's hands in hers. "You're not ruining anything." She squeezed her fingers reassuringly. "I don't know exactly what happened between you and Sam, but I know that four years is a long time. He hasn't married. You haven't married. That tells me more than either one of you could."

Olivia's eyes widened as she began to see the wheels clicking inside Kathleen's head. "Kathleen, you're crazy! The man would like nothing better than to throw me into the hog pen!"

Kathleen began to laugh. "My dear Olivia, it's almost Thanksgiving, a time of family, home and love. It's a time when people are drawn back together to say I love you and I'm so thankful to have you in my life. My quiet, dependable brother will come round. You can count on it."

Olivia shook her head. Sam was a strong-minded man. He wouldn't bend. He wouldn't forgive. Even if it was a holiday to remember one's blessings. "The only thing I'm going to count on, Kathleen, is that Ella has turkey and candied sweet potatoes on the Thanksgiving dinner table."

Chapter Six

Sam wasn't hungry. He didn't even know why he continued to sit at the supper table, pushing his food from one side of his plate to the other. The only reason he'd come down in the first place was so that he would appear normal to the rest of the family. Even if he didn't feel normal.

And how could any man feel normal, he wondered, with a woman like Olivia sitting only a few inches away? She'd changed her clothes from the jeans she'd had on earlier this afternoon at the barn. Now she had on a V-necked cranberry-colored sweater, and even though he couldn't see the lower half of her now, he'd seen enough before she sat down to give him plenty to think about.

The gathered skirt she had on was long, covering the tops of her suede boots, but the material was a soft, clingy sort that cuddled her bottom like a gloved hand. She was the most desirable woman Sam had ever seen, and it infuriated him because he still wanted her. Wanted her with every breath he took.

Sam's thoughts were interrupted when S.T. rose from his seat at the end of the table. "Well, I guess two platefuls should be enough to do me for a while. I'm going over to Fred Dunaway's to look at his new pickup truck. Wanta come, Ma?" he asked Ella.

Ella shook her head at her husband. "I still have too much cooking to do. You go on without me."

"Mother, go with him," Kathleen urged. "Lillian will be disappointed if you don't go to see her. It would be a good time to take her and Fred some of that pumpkin bread you've been making."

"Well, I would like to see her and wish her a happy Thanksgiving," Ella said of her friend who lived over near Van Buren.

Seeing her mother's hesitation, Kathleen went on, "Olivia and I can do whatever needs doing. Daddy would like your company."

Frowning, Ella rose from the table, gathering dirty dishes as she did. "But there's so much I need to do yet. Pecans to crack, and corn bread to make for the stuffing and—"

S.T. reached out and snaked an arm around his wife's waist to prevent her from making a trip to the kitchen sink. "Kathleen's right, gal. So go get your coat. I'll wait for you at the yard gate."

"Ooh, Mother, you'd better hurry," Kathleen said in a teasing voice. "Sounds like Daddy's getting romantic."

"Romantic, my foot," Ella said with a snort. "In thirty-degree weather all S.T. needs is an electric blanket."

"We'll see about that," S.T. said, propelling his wife out of the kitchen with a swat on her bottom.

The couple's warm repartee put a sad little smile on Olivia's face. Her parents had never been openly affectionate with each other: she'd only ever seen them exchange proper little pecks on the cheek. Now that Olivia thought about it, those little demonstrations had probably been for her benefit, to make her believe her parents were in love. Olivia seriously doubted either of them had ever been in love with each other. The Wescotts were married to each other because it was financially and socially advantageous for both of them.

She looked over at Sam, who was quietly sipping his coffee. Did he know how lucky he was to have parents who really loved each other? Or was he so used to having a loving family around him that he took it all for granted?

Olivia rose from her chair and began gathering the dirty plates and cups from the table. "I'm glad you talked Ella into going with S.T. She needs a break from this kitchen. The way she's been going at it, she'll be exhausted by the time Thanksgiving Day arrives."

Kathleen placed her coffee cup with the stack of dishes Olivia had already gathered. "Dad will keep her over at Fred and Lillian's for hours, so we should be able to get a lot of things done before she gets back." She rose to her feet, then waved a hand to shoo Olivia away from the table. "Leave the dishes to me, I have another chore I need for you to do."

"Kathleen, you know that you're much better at cooking than I am. I should do the dishes."

"I'm not cooking," Kathleen quickly assured her. She looked at her brother as put his coffee cup aside. "We need a big pumpkin to cook and puree for pies. Will you go pick out a nice one? Sam will show you where they are, won't you, dear brother?"

Sam, who'd appeared indifferent to the whole conversation, was now suddenly frowning at his sister. "You don't need a pumpkin tonight. You'll have all day tomorrow to cook pumpkin."

Kathleen merely smiled at her brother. Olivia wanted to scream. She didn't want to be thrown at Sam any more than he wanted her thrown at him. She just hoped to God he didn't realize what his sister was doing, because Olivia certainly did. And she could have told the other woman it wasn't going to work.

"Listen, buster, if you want pie, you'll get off your can and take Olivia down to the root cellar," Kathleen told him.

"Take me down to the root cellar?" Olivia repeated jokingly. "That sounds like something out of a horror novel."

Kathleen laughed as she whisked an armful of dirty dishes over to the kitchen sink. "Don't worry, Olivia. Sam might look menacing, but he won't really hurt you."

I wouldn't bet on that, Kathleen. Olivia let out a long, surrendering breath and looked over at Sam, who was still seated at the table, even though he'd finished the last of his coffee. He wasn't looking at her, but Olivia knew he was just as much aware of her as she was of him.

"Just tell me where they are, Sam. I can find one." Without your help, Olivia felt like adding.

He could hear the pride in her voice and knew she didn't want his help or his company. She was an independent woman, one who hadn't needed him or his love. He supposed he should have seen that about her long ago, but he'd been blinded by his feelings. Now he was seeing her with his eyes open, and he planned to keep them that way.

Slowly he lifted his head to meet her gaze. There was a faint challenge in her blue eyes. It heated his blood almost as much as the memory of their kiss this afternoon in the barn. Sam hadn't meant for that to happen. He hadn't meant to touch her, or to like it so much. But he had. Now he couldn't get her or what she'd said out of his mind.

With two big fists he pushed his chair away from the supper table and rose to his feet. "I doubt it. We buried them under hay and burlap. I'll get a flashlight and take you."

Sam left the room and Olivia made fast tracks to the kitchen sink, where Kathleen was already up to her elbows in soapy dishwater. "All right, Kathleen." Olivia's voice was low and threatening. "What do you think you're doing? If you think you can matchmake me and Sam back together you're out of your mind!"

Kathleen's expression was a picture of innocence. "Aren't you being overly dramatic, Olivia? I merely asked you to go after a pumpkin, not after my brother. Unless you want to, that is," she added, a coy grin suddenly transforming her face.

Groaning, Olivia threw up her hands. "I suppose you think you can cure me, just like you thought you could cure that poor guy of having the hives? Well, let me tell you that you'll be just about as successful!"

Kathleen laughed softly. "What am I supposed to be curing you of?"

Knowing Kathleen was goading her flustered Olivia even more. "You know what! Of—of—"

Her words came to an abrupt halt as Sam stepped back into the room. He'd pulled on a brown work coat and a cap that had a tractor insignia on the front. A large flashlight was in his right hand.

"Go get your coat, Olivia. I'll meet you at the gate," he told her.

Just when Olivia had assured herself she could remain indifferent to the man, he had to go and say something like that. Didn't he realize his father had said nearly the very same words to his mother only minutes ago? But there's a big difference now, Olivia, she told herself. S.T. loves Ella and wants her company. Whereas Sam is merely doing a chore. Reluctantly at that.

The night was very cold and still as Olivia walked across the crisp brown grass in the backyard. Sometime during the evening clouds had moved in to cover the sky. Like a heavy quilt, they darkened the night and put a hint of moisture in the air.

"Do you think it might snow?" Olivia asked as she reached the gate where Sam was waiting.

"I doubt it," he said. "But you never know."

Switching on the flashlight, he pointed a path through the darkness. Without touching him, Olivia stayed close to his side as they began to walk.

"I haven't seen snow in a long time. It would be lovely if we had a white Christmas this year."

Sam was beginning to realize more and more just how much Olivia had given up while she'd been away. He wondered if she regretted it. Or was her pride in all the work she'd done and the lives she'd saved more important than what she'd missed?

"I thought you weren't going to be here in Arkansas for Christmas. At least, that's what you told Kathleen."

Olivia knew that's what she had implied. It was much easier than having to explain she was too used up to go back to Africa.

Used up. Is that what she was? she wondered. She didn't know anymore. She only knew her spirit felt dead and she was ashamed for anyone to know it. Especially Sam.

"Well, I'm not quite certain where I'll be during Christmas. I just didn't want to make Kathleen a promise I couldn't keep."

Sam had been telling himself he wished Olivia were anywhere but here on the farm, wished she were having Thanksgiving with anyone but him. But he knew that wasn't quite true. Just to think of her not being here in a few days tore a gaping hole in him, one that became a bleeding wound. It didn't make sense. But then nothing about him and Olivia made any sense at all.

"She said that you'd been ill."

"I wish she hadn't told you that," Olivia said grimly.

"Why?"

"I don't want anyone to cosset or pity me."

"You won't get that from a Gallagher. But you will get concern."

She turned her head just enough to look up at him. "From you? I find that hard to believe."

He took her arm as the ground grew rougher. Olivia felt her heart kick into overdrive. Not only at his touch, but also at the look on his face. There was no mockery twisting his mouth, no blame or resentment hardening his brown eyes.

"Are you all right now, Olivia?"

Something in her turned over at the tender sound of his voice. "Not quite. But I'm getting close to it."

The pressure of his hand on her arm halted her steps. Olivia felt her insides begin to quiver and melt as his thumb and forefinger lifted her chin and forced her to face him.

"What is it? Were you . . . seriously ill?"

She couldn't lie to him. He was too much a part of her to ever lie to him. "For a while. You see, I was helping out in a makeshift hospital that had been set up in the camp where we'd been distributing food. Some sort of fever had swept through two of the settlements near there, and we were trying to help as best we could. I thought I'd been immunized against that particular strain, but it turned out I wasn't. Before I knew it, I was lying in a cot freezing and sweating along with the others."

Just the image of Olivia in those conditions made Sam want to gather her into his arms and hold her safe against his heart. To never let her go. "Didn't you have medication to deal with the disease?"

She nodded. "Enough for me to get over the roughest part of it. But since my job forces me to live and work under harsh conditions, my body couldn't recuperate as quickly as the doctors wished. So..." She shrugged and tried to smile. "They sent me back here."

"That must have been a blow for you. Being forced to leave your work."

No, she thought, it hadn't really been a blow, but rather the final straw that had broken her back. She'd known for quite a few months that she was going to have to leave Africa. She'd known that her heart, her spirit couldn't take any more. But she'd put off leaving. Because she'd known there was nothing here in the States to come home to.

Her illness had forced her to make a choice.

"No one likes to admit that they're weak," Olivia told him.

With his hand still on her arm, Sam guided her forward. "Even the strongest get sick from time to time, Olivia."

A few steps ahead of them, Olivia could see what appeared to be a cellar. Sod had been pushed up around it, making a mound of earth on the otherwise flat ground.

Sam pulled open the heavy door, then reached for Olivia's hand. "Better let me help you," he said. "These steps are steep and there isn't any light down here."

She gave him her hand and his warm grip swallowed it up. She thought of how strong he was and how, if he had to, he would use that strength to protect a woman. He was that sort of man. A quiet, powerful man whose emotions ran deep. She hadn't realized just how deep until she'd seen him again.

"I thought people used cellars to protect themselves from tornadoes," Olivia said as the two of them descended steep concrete steps.

"We've used this one as a storm shelter, too. But it's a good place to store vegetables that Mom doesn't freeze or can." He placed the flashlight on a shelf near the entrance. It provided enough light to illuminate the enclosure with a dim glow.

The ceiling was low, forcing Sam to duck his head; however, Olivia was short enough to stand upright. She could see that two-thirds of the floor was covered with a pile of hay at least waist high. It was no wonder Sam had given in and made the trip down here with her. She wouldn't have had the slightest idea of where to begin digging.

He let go of her hand and Olivia decided she should move back and give him space enough to work. However, he caught her shoulder just as she started to step away. She looked up at him, her eyes questioning.

One corner of his mouth lifted ruefully. "I...just wanted to say I'm glad you're getting well."

His words and the genuine concern in his eyes were like a hand squeezing her heart. "Coming from you, that's quite an admission. I figured it would have made you happy to see me fail."

He frowned with disbelief. "Fail? Olivia, just because you became ill doesn't mean you're a failure."

But she was a failure. He just didn't know it yet, she thought sadly. And how could she tell him? she wondered. How could she tell him that she'd failed so badly that she couldn't go back to Africa? In fact, she didn't know if she would ever be able to do relief work again.

She'd given up Sam's love for her ideal of saving lives. Now that ideal was gone. And so was Sam's love. It was almost more than she could bear.

"Maybe not," she said, then she looked away from him and blinked her eyes. For God's sake, she couldn't cry! Not again!

"After you left I worried that something would happen to you," he said. "I didn't think you'd be strong enough to last a month. Instead you were gone four years. That's a hell of a long time, Olivia."

What was he saying? That he missed her? Had he counted the days, the months, the years, the same way she had? She didn't think so. After all, he hadn't even bothered to read her letters. He'd returned them just as she'd sent them, the envelope untouched, her words of love meaning no more to him than scratches of ink on a piece of paper. Each time a letter had come back to her, it had been as if Sam slapped her in the face. Finally the pain had been too great and she'd quit trying to reach him.

Olivia looked up at him. "In some ways, I guess it has been a long time." But she'd thought about him every one of those days, wondering if he'd found someone else to take her place in his heart, wondering, too, if he ever thought of her at all. "I know I feel much older now."

Sam's eyes scanned her oval face, searching the tender lines and angles that made up her delicate features. He couldn't say the past four years had aged her face. But her eyes had changed. That spark that had once fired them to the color of glowing sapphires was gone, leaving them flat and lifeless. Sam had seen that same look in Kathleen's eyes when she'd lost her husband.

It didn't make sense, he thought. Olivia had been ill, but she hadn't lost anyone. At least not that he knew of. "This morning you said you'd come close to being engaged. What happened?"

Her eyes fell away from his. "No more than what I told your mother and sister. We were just good friends, pretending to be more. It didn't work."

Jealousy raked through him, even though he knew it was stupid to feel such an emotion. "Did he work with you?"

She nodded. "For a year. He left after things didn't work out between us. But we parted as friends." Not hissing and snarling like she and Sam had, she thought. She pulled her eyes back to his face. "What about you, Sam? Why haven't you married?"

Didn't she know? Wasn't it written all over his face? His mind and heart had been so filled with her that he could never make room in them for anyone else. What few times he'd tried had been almost painful. He didn't want to look at a woman, touch a woman, unless it was the one he loved. And the one he loved was Olivia. He knew that now just as strongly as he'd known it four years ago. He just didn't know what to do about it anymore.

"Because I haven't wanted to," he said, turning toward the stack of hay. "We'd better find that pumpkin and get back to the house. It's cold down here."

Olivia was anything but cold. Having Sam so close and knowing they were completely alone was doing strange things to her. She wanted to reach out to him. Throw away her pride and beg him to kiss her, to make love to her.

She nodded numbly, even though he was no longer looking at her. "Yes, you're right. Kathleen probably needs our help."

Sam selected the largest pumpkin in the nest, then covered the remainder with a heavy blanket of hay. Olivia fetched the flashlight from the shelf and guided their way out of the cellar.

The night air seemed to have grown even colder. As they walked back to the house Olivia found herself inching closer to the warmth of Sam's body.

"I want to thank you, Sam."

"For what?"

Her free hand closed lightly around his forearm. "For not saying I told you so."

Her hand was just a tiny little thing on his arm, yet it caused an upheaval inside him. He continued to walk, although he kept his stride slower to match hers. "And when were you expecting me to say that?"

"When I told you about my illness. God knows you tried to warn me before I left for Africa."

It was true he'd warned her. Hell, he'd done more than warned her. He'd threatened her, cajoled her, tried to reason with her any way he could to keep her from going to Africa. He just hadn't pleaded with her. He'd had too much pride to beg her to stay.

"Saying I told you so wouldn't give me any satisfaction, Olivia. Maybe two or three months after you left it would have. But not now."

In other words it was too late, Olivia told herself. He no longer cared. Somehow she'd known that, but still her heart just didn't want to accept it.

Back in the kitchen, Olivia and Kathleen cleaned the pumpkin of seeds and rind, then cut it into stewing-size pieces. Once it was simmering in a huge pot over a low flame Kathleen began to look for the pecans Ella wanted shelled.

She found them in the utility room among the laundry detergent and garden seed. "I'm pretty sure these are the fresh ones," Kathleen said. "Daddy got them last month when he and Mother went to see my uncle. There's nothing like East Texas pecans, he always says."

She handed the bag and a nutcracker to Olivia. "Why don't you take these into the den, and I'll get a bowl to put the nuts in. We'll throw the shells into the fire."

Olivia left the kitchen and crossed the breezeway. When she entered the den, she saw Sam sitting at a desk in the corner of the room. He was busily working at a computer, until he heard the sound of her footsteps. Then he turned and looked over his shoulder.

He said nothing and neither did she. But Olivia could feel his eyes follow her as she moved to the fireplace.

Lowering herself to the floor, she placed the sack of nuts on the rock hearth, then curled her legs up beneath the swirl of her skirt. "If you're working, don't let me disturb you," she said, feeling the need to break the awkward silence.

He'd been going through the motions of working. But so far the computer screen hadn't managed to distract him from the images running through his mind. "I was just going over a few tax deductions for this last quarter."

Reaching forward, he pushed a few buttons and the computer screen went black. Olivia wondered if he was foregoing his work out of politeness or if he was simply telling her she'd interrupted him.

"I can go back to the kitchen if my being here disturbs your train of thought," she felt compelled to say.

She couldn't possibly know just how much she did disturb him, or that she'd been disturbing his thoughts long before she entered the room.

Shaking his head, Sam said, "I was almost finished anyway. Besides, I hate working on these damn things."

Without having to ask, Olivia knew he was talking about the computer. "I take it you'd rather be on a tractor."

"Any time," he told her. "But farming isn't just plowing ground and planting seeds. It's a business. And like most businesses it has plenty of paperwork to keep up with."

"My job didn't require any paperwork. So now that I'm back in the States I have to remind myself to pay the utilities and balance my checkbook. It's wearisome."

His gaze leveled on her face. "Which one? The paperwork or being back in the States?"

"The paperwork. As for being back in the States, it feels good." It just didn't feel like home, she thought. An apartment in Little Rock wasn't the same as a house filled with loving, caring relatives.

When he didn't reply, Olivia took a handful of large pecans from the sack and placed one between the jaws of the tool in her hand. "We finally got the pumpkin cooking," she said, keeping her eyes on her task. "We'll probably have enough pureed pumpkin to make twenty pies. Did you grow them here on the farm?"

He nodded, then, realizing she wasn't looking at him, said, "Mom grew them in the vegetable garden. Amazing how abundant Mother Nature is. I think Mom planted only two or three vines, but it was enough to have pumpkins running out our ears."

Olivia reached for another pecan. "I suppose with the right kind of soil and weather, and tools, a person can grow food aplenty. I only wish it could be that way in Ethiopia and other countries plagued with famine."

She pressed down on the handles of the nutcracker until the pecan shell crunched. Sam watched her slow methodical movements as his mind replayed the conversation they'd had in the barn. She'd gone so far as to admit that because of her parents' rich, wasteful life-style, she'd wanted to be a relief worker. But was that the reason she'd continued for four long years? He'd heard of people committing a year or two out of their lives for such a cause, but damn it, Olivia had given that much of her life two or three times over.

"Not every country in the world is blessed with farmland like we have here in the States," he said. "And even if it was, a person has to have capital and know-how to raise a crop."

Just as Olivia glanced over at him, Kathleen breezed into the room carrying a plastic bowl. "What's this? Are you giving Olivia one of your farming-ecology speeches?"

Groaning inwardly, Sam reached to switch off the desk lamp. His restlessness last night had left him bone tired, but he knew if he went upstairs to his bed he wouldn't be able to sleep.

"And what if I am?" he asked his sister.

Kathleen gave her brother a pointed look. "This is a holiday, Sam. A time for happiness and celebration. Can't you ever lighten up?"

"It's not his fault," Olivia interrupted. "I was the one who brought up the subject." She shook her head ruefully at Kathleen's surprised expression. "It's . . . hard for me to forget that there are people out there who won't be eating a wonderful Thanksgiving dinner like the one we'll have. In fact, they won't be eating at all."

Kathleen's reply was to reach over and pat Olivia's hand. Sam didn't say anything. The sight of Olivia's bent head was cutting a path straight to his heart. She honestly cared. It really was hurting her to know that there were people out there who needed help, food, shelter.

God, how could he ever have thought otherwise? he asked himself.

Because it had been easier that way, he answered. It had eased his ache and his bitterness to believe that she cared only about herself, and about making everyone see her as some sort of self-sacrificing angel.

Forcing a bright smile on her face, Olivia went back to cracking pecans. "But you are right, Kathleen. Now is a time for being happy and thankful. And if you're going to be eating Ella's cooking, it's not a time to be worrying about counting calories."

"Amen to that," Kathleen said with a chuckle, then patted her flat tummy. "I always gain five pounds over the holidays! Of course Sam over there can eat like a hog and never gain an ounce. When God handed out metabolisms, Sam got lucky."

Olivia glanced across the room to where Sam was getting to his feet. His brooding expression was suddenly transformed by a cocky little grin. "Lucky?" he said with a snort. "It's hard work that keeps the fat off me. Not luck or metabolism."

"Hmm. Well, if you're such a worker, get over here and help us with these nuts. After all, you are the one who wanted a pecan pie," Kathleen reminded teasingly.

Olivia expected him to come up with a quick excuse to leave the room, and was totally surprised when he crossed the room to join them.

"What can I do?" he asked, squatting down on his heels beside the two women. "I've only got one good hand."

"You can squeeze with it, can't you?" Kathleen asked.

The chuckle he gave was faint, but Olivia heard it and was warmed by the sound. The Sam she'd first fallen in love with had been a quiet man, but he'd been a happy one. She wanted to see that Sam again. She wanted to believe that somehow she hadn't ruined his life, even if she had ruined her own.

"I've got a grip our brother Nick would kill for," he said, reaching to take the nutcracker from Olivia.

Their fingers awkwardly collided as they made the exchange. Olivia felt a heat that had nothing to do with the fireplace course through her body. In spite of it, she lifted her eyes to meet his.

Sam felt his mouth go dry as his eyes drifted down to linger on her pink pouty lips. He could feast on those lips for hours and still not get enough of her, he realized.

"Nick might have a thing or two to say about that," Kathleen said, her attention on the pecan she was shelling.

His sister's voice pulled Sam back to the present and he lowered himself to the floor beside the two women. "Oh yeah, brother Nick will put up an argument," he agreed.

"He'll do more than that. He'll challenge you to an arm-wrestling duel. At least ten or twelve times."

"All of which I'll have to win."

Kathleen gave her brother a knowing look. "You mean half of them, don't you?"

Olivia placed the sack of nuts where Sam could easily reach them, and he began to squash them effortlessly between the metal jaws in his hand.

"Well, you know I have to let Nick win the other half or his ego would suffer."

Kathleen hooted with laughter and Olivia found herself smiling. The Sam she'd known would never brag. It was amusing to see him even try to do it jokingly.

"Where is your brother now?" Olivia asked, leaving the question open to either one of them.

"Fort Sill," Sam answered.

"And we haven't seen him since Easter. I can hardly wait for him to come home," Kathleen explained. "And if he doesn't call and let us know something by tomorrow, Mother is going to be wringing her hands."

"That's true enough," Sam said. "She's close to calling his captain as it is, and demanding that he let her son come home for Thanksgiving."

Olivia's gaze encompassed both Sam and Kathleen. They each favored their tall, dark-headed mother. She couldn't remember too much about Nick Gallagher other than that he'd been a big tease. "You don't know how lucky you are to have a mother like Ella. I can't think of anyone with a more loving, giving heart than her."

Kathleen suddenly gasped. "Oh, heavens, speaking of Mother, she's going to kill me if she gets back and there's no corn bread baked for dressing. And we have to have the food we're donating to the church drive ready to go by ten tomorrow morning." She tossed the nuts she was holding into the plastic bowl and jumped to her feet. "I'll go whip up a batch before she and Daddy get back here."

"Do you need help?" Olivia asked.

Kathleen was already on her way out of the den. "No. You and Sam just keep on doing what you're doing."

The room went quiet without Kathleen in it. The only sound to be heard was the hissing of the fire and the cracking of pecan shells.

After a few moments Olivia glanced over at Sam. He must have sensed that she was looking at him because he lifted his head and leveled his brown eyes on hers. Olivia felt a strange tightening in the pit of her stomach.

"The house would be very quiet without Kathleen or your parents."

"In a few months I'll be finding out just how quiet," he replied.

Her brows lifted with curiosity. "Oh? Why is that?"

Sam looked back down at the nutcracker in his hand. "Mom and Dad are moving to Texas this spring. They've already bought a house close to Dad's brother."

Olivia was very surprised. Even though she knew that Sam had taken over the running of the farm, she had expected his parents to still make their home here.

"I hadn't realized that."

She dug pecan halves out of their shells, then tossed them into the bowl, which was slowing filling up.

"Are you . . . looking forward to having the place all to yourself?" she asked.

He didn't answer immediately. Olivia looked over at him just in time to see him shrug his shoulders. "I doubt my lifestyle will change, if that's what you're asking," he said tersely.

Olivia pitched a handful of empty shells over her shoulder and into the dancing flames in the fireplace. "I wasn't really expecting you to start having all-night orgies, Sam."

A grin spread slowly across his face. Olivia's eyes were drawn to his sensual mouth, the whiteness of his teeth, the darkness of his skin.

He was a rugged, earthy man, the type that had no problem attracting women. Yet she knew he was a man too deeply motivated to have careless or casual affairs. But would the loneliness of an empty house force him to seek out the companionship of a woman?

"Well, maybe just half-the-night orgies," he drawled.

Olivia knew he was joking. Even so, she was consumed with jealousy. She couldn't bear to think of Sam touching another woman the way he'd touched her, kissing another woman the way he'd kissed her.

While she'd been in Africa she'd told herself she wanted Sam to get married, to find a woman who would truly make him happy. But looking at him now, she knew it would have killed her to have come back to the Gallagher farm and found him with a wife and children.

Oh God, what am I doing? This man doesn't love me. I killed that love when I chose to go to Africa. So why can't I get him out of my mind? Why do I keep trying to look inside him, hoping I'll see that his heart has changed?

"After all," she heard him continue, "I'm pretty hayseed. I don't know that much about wild partying."

He was anything but hayseed. They both knew that.

She went back to the task of shelling pecans. "I expected you to have children by now."

This time Olivia was the one who felt his gaze burning over her. She lifted her eyes to his, then felt her pulse lurch into a drunken, erratic beat. His face had a strangely wounded expression, as if she'd touched the very core of his heart.

"So did I, Olivia. But you weren't here to give them to me."

Chapter Seven

Olivia stood in her gown and robe, staring out the window of her bedroom. Hours had come and gone since she and Sam had shelled pecans by the fire. But the time had not lessened the impact of his words.

Sam had expected to have children with her. And because she'd gone away, he had none.

Lord, it had been a blessing that Ella and S.T. had chosen that moment to return home and enter the den with a noisy burst of conversation. Otherwise, Olivia didn't know what she would have done or said.

Would she have argued with him, tried to make him see that their parting hadn't been solely her fault? Or would she have simply burst into tears and fled the room?

Sighing heavily, Olivia looked out across the barren fields. A heavy mist had begun to fall, shrouding the night sky with a milky fog. Far off in the darkness she could see the lights of a river barge slowly making its way upstream to Oklahoma.

It was a lonely sight, made even lonelier by the ache in Olivia's heart.

Hugging her arms around her slender waist, she walked back to the bedside. It was after midnight. She should have been asleep by now, but too many questions, too many memories kept roiling around in her mind.

A small photo album was on the square nightstand by her bed. Earlier Olivia had taken the book out of her suitcase and gone through some of the scenes she'd snapped during her work in Ethiopia.

Impulsively, she reached for it again and began to leaf through the pages. She'd brought the album with her, thinking she would show it to Kathleen and Ella. Many of the snapshots were of fellow workers and the barracks-style housing she'd lived in. Others were more telling—of hungry faces beside a crude shack, of children too weak to feed themselves.

Olivia had believed that over time she would able to deal with the suffering; that she could see it, live with it and still keep her feelings detached. But it hadn't worked that way. Seeing the tragedy day after day for four years had broken her spirit. It was no wonder, she thought, that the fever had hit her so hard. She'd had nothing left in her with which to fight it.

A soft knock on the door startled Olivia out of her dismal musings. Placing the book on the bed, she crossed the room, wondering who could possibly be up at this hour.

She was shocked to find Sam on the other side of the door. He was shirtless and his feet were bare. The rest of him was covered with a pair of old jeans.

"Sam? Is . . . something wrong?"

He swallowed as his eyes left her face and drifted slowly down the length of her. Her hair was loose around her neck and shoulders, and she was wearing that peachy thing again. It outlined the shape of her breasts and the curve of her hips in a subtle but tempting way. Sam wondered once again why she had to be so damn beautiful, so unbelievably desirable.

"Er, no. Not really." He frowned, silently wishing he hadn't knocked on her door. He was having enough trouble sleeping as it was. "I just..." He held up the hand he'd cut yesterday. "The bandage came loose when I showered and I tried to fix it. But I couldn't make much headway with just one hand."

"You want me to bandage it again for you?"

He shifted uncomfortably. "Well, you're the only who's awake."

For some crazy reason, she felt disappointed. For a second, when she'd opened the door and seen him standing there, she'd thought he'd come to her because he wanted her. Not just her help.

Shaking away the foolish notion, she pushed the door aside for him to enter. "Of course I'll bandage it for you. Do you have the gauze and tape with you?"

He stepped inside, his eyes taking a quick survey of her things scattered around the room. A bottle of perfume on the dresser, a silky black slip carelessly draped over a wooden rocking chair. Funny how two days ago this had been merely an extra bedroom. Now he thought of it as *her* room.

To answer her question, he extended the first-aid kit. Olivia took it, then motioned toward the lamp on the nightstand. The only light burning in the room, it created a soft, rosy glow over part of the bed.

"Why don't we go over here under the light?" she suggested.

Sam picked up a dressing bench from the foot of the bed and followed her over to the light. Olivia took a seat on the edge of the bed, while Sam sat down on the padded bench. Their knees bumped in the process, making Olivia jerk back as though she'd been grazed by a hot wire.

She knew it was stupid to react so physically to him. He just wanted his hand bandaged. The fact that they were alone in her bedroom while the rest of the household slept was probably the last thing on his mind.

Still, it was a struggle for Olivia to keep her hands from shaking as she opened the first-aid kit.

"I shouldn't have bothered you with this," Sam said suddenly. "I-it could have waited till tomorrow."

Tucking her loose hair behind her ears, Olivia reached for his hand. "It would be dangerous to leave it uncovered. All sorts of bacteria could get into it and cause infection."

Her hands were soft and infinitely gentle as they touched him. Sam suddenly forgot how stiff and sore his fingers were as she laid his hand upon her lap. He could feel the warmth of her legs beneath the thin silky fabric, smell the flowery sweetness of her hair as she bent over his cradled hand.

Sam drew in a long breath, let it out, then tried to speak normally. "It's been a long time since I've had a cut or burn. I'd forgotten what a nuisance they can be."

Olivia gently massaged his palm to lessen the stiffness he might feel when she uncurled his hand. "You're lucky that you still have these two fingers. That tin could have sliced them off completely.

"Yeah. You're probably right."

She dabbed antiseptic on a cotton swab and gently cleaned the edges of the wound. It was bittersweet for Olivia to be touching him this way, to be able to do something personal for him.

"Your mom and dad seemed to have had a good time tonight," she said conversationally.

"Fred and Lillian have been close friends for years. They have a little farm over near Van Buren. Fred raises milo and a few cattle."

"Ella seemed pleased with all we got done while she was away. She'll be taking the food to the church tomorrow. She was especially happy with the pecans. Shelling them is so time-consuming," Olivia went on, afraid that if she didn't keep talking she'd lose every scrap of her composure.

"Mom always looks forward to cooking for the holidays."

"And you look forward to eating," she said, her voice softly teasing.

He wished she would hurry. If he didn't get out of here, he was going to say something, do something he would regret.

Hell, he already had. Sam silently cursed himself. He should have never said that to her about having children. He didn't know why he had, except that it had been the truth, and for Sam, evading the truth was a hard thing to do.

Olivia found the gauze, then began slowing wrapping it around Sam's hand. Part of her was relieved the job was nearly over. Yet a more foolish part of her wanted to dally, to keep him with her as long as she possibly could.

"Sam, I know that you didn't—" she swallowed and tried again "—you didn't want me here for Thanksgiving. But I...well, being with your family is so nice. I'm glad you didn't insist that I leave."

Her words couldn't have surprised him more. "Why would you think I could do such a thing?"

Sam's softly spoken question pulled her head up. She realized then just how close they were to each other, so close she could see the texture of his lips, the gold flecks in his brown eyes. Her heart moved into a dizzying gallop.

"Because," she said, her voice a hoarse whisper, "you hate me."

She thought he hated her? Stunned, Sam stared at her. "Olivia..."

Tears rushed to her eyes. She quickly dropped her head, hoping he hadn't seen them. "You don't have to say anything, Sam. Now that I've had time to think about it, I know... that I made a mess of things all those years ago. I thought that if you loved me, you would automatically share my ideals."

She shook her head, then forced herself to look back up at him. From the frown on his face, she knew he was trying to make some sort of meaning from her words.

Sam was only partially aware she'd quit wrapping the gauze and was now simply holding on to his hand. He was still dazed that she could think he hated her. Sam had never hated another human being in his life. True, Olivia had hurt him, but hate was nowhere near the emotion he felt for her. He felt anger and desire. He felt frustration and bitterness, but never hate.

"It wasn't your ideals I was against, Olivia. Whatever you might think, I have compassion for people who are less fortunate than me."

Somehow Olivia had always known that—that deep down, Sam was a man who cared about other people, perhaps even more than he cared about himself. If not, it would never have mattered to him that more than a hundred years ago his ancestors had worked and struggled to make this farm into a home.

Drawing in a shaky breath, she looked back down at his hand and forced her trembling fingers to finish tying the bandage. "There. That should fix you up for a while."

She didn't look at him as she packed the articles back into the first-aid box. Frustrated because she seemed to be dismissing him, Sam said, "You don't believe me? You don't believe that I care about starving or homeless people?"

"I believe that you do. Just not in the same way that I do."

"I didn't become a relief worker like you did," he conceded gruffly. "If that's what you mean."

"Hmm. Well, you believe I became one only to thwart my parents."

Sam had promised himself after that episode in the barn that he wasn't going to let her rile him again. But he could feel a rush of anger rising up in him, pushing hot blood to his temples with each beat of his heart.

"You so much as admitted it. Didn't you?"

She made a helpless gesture with her hands, then glanced up at him. "Yes, I did. For as long as I can remember, I've resented their rich, self-absorbed life-style. Somehow I wanted to make up for their shortcomings. But that wasn't the only reason I went to Africa."

"What was the other reason?" he asked.

Had it been because of him? Sam wondered. Had she figured going halfway around the world was the best way to get away from him and his proposal of marriage?

That he had to ask incensed Olivia. Before she realized what she was doing, she reached for the photo album lying among the tousled bed covers.

Wordlessly, she handed the book to him.

Frowning quizzically, Sam took it, then allowed it to fall open. Pictures of Olivia jumped out at him. His fingers tightened on the edge of the plastic-laminated sheets as he found himself staring at a woman he knew, yet didn't know. In nearly all of them she was dressed in khaki shorts or pants and simple tank tops. Her blond hair was pulled back into either a ponytail or a braid. She wore no makeup, no jewelry. Yet those superficial things were not what really caught Sam's eye. Rather it was the compassion on her face as she spooned food into a toddler's mouth, the grim determination in her expression as she helped unload a truck of supplies in the African heat.

Sam had seen tragic scenes such as these on television, of course. But it was altogether different seeing Olivia in such conditions. It made everything so much closer, so much more real to him. And it made him wonder if four years ago he had misjudged her. Certainly he hadn't understood her.

Mesmerized, he found it impossible not to turn the pages. He felt he had to keep looking, as though one more picture might tell him something about her that she wouldn't or couldn't reveal herself.

Suddenly her finger touched the page in front of him. His gaze followed its direction to a photo of Olivia holding a child in her arms. From the looks of the boy, Sam doubted he could have been more than three years old.

"This child's mother," she said quietly, "carried him twenty miles to our camp. He was suffering from extreme malnutrition, dysentery and dehydration."

"Did he survive?"

Olivia's fingers curled into tight little fists at her sides as a myriad of emotions rained over her. For some reason that particular child had touched a spot in her that no other had. She'd vowed to save him, and for two weeks she'd worked feverishly along with a medical aid to care for him. Yet it had been too little, too late. He'd died, and something in Olivia had died along with him.

She was silent for so long that Sam began to think she wasn't going to answer. When she finally did, her voice was harsh, almost bitter. "No. He didn't make it."

Sam lifted his gaze from the collage of photos. Olivia's face was turned away from him, yet they were sitting so close to each other that he could see the rigid line of her jaw, the trickle of tears running from the corner of her closed eye.

The sight ripped him open, and he reached for her hands, folding them between his. He wanted so badly to comfort her, to say something that would take the tortured look from her face. But he didn't know what to say that wouldn't sound trite. Even a blind man could see that Olivia had suffered not only physically from her stay in Ethiopia, she'd also suffered emotionally.

In that moment Sam realized he didn't want her to go back. He didn't want her to be torn apart by a world problem that was far too big for her small shoulders. But what right did he have to ask her to stay? She was obviously still committed to her cause. And she'd told him in plain words that their past relationship was nothing more than a memory to her.

"I'm sure you tried your best to help him."

His low, gentle voice should have soothed her, but as Olivia turned her head toward him, all she could think of was the utter waste her efforts had been.

"But my best wasn't good enough, Sam."

Before he could stop her she jumped up from the bed and crossed the room. At the window, her back to him, she folded her arms around her waist in a self-protective gesture.

Sam left his place on the bench, and moving behind her, placed his hand on her shoulder. "Olivia, there will be other children. Children that you *will* save."

Tears clogged her throat as she thought about that lost African child, and even more, she thought about the children that she and Sam could have had but never would.

"No." She couldn't go back to Africa. She couldn't go through another year, another month or even a day of living on her emotions, of giving too much of herself, and not having anyone to hold her, to love her and fill her back up again.

His fingers tightened on the slope of her shoulder. "What do you mean, no?"

Olivia hadn't meant to say the word. But being this close to Sam, having him touching her, numbed her common sense. "I just meant that...well, whatever I do in the future won't bring that child back."

The future. For some reason Sam didn't want to think about the future. In two or three days Olivia would be gone, on the way to her apartment in Little Rock. And no doubt in a few weeks, when she was determined physically fit by her doctor, she would be flying back to Africa. He probably wouldn't see her again for another four years. Or maybe not ever. How was he going to live with that?

"Olivia, none of us can ever go back and change our pasts."

Tears burned her throat. How she wished she could go back to when she and Sam had shared those few short weeks together. Those days had been the happiest in her life. Why hadn't she been able to see that she needed Sam and a home much more than she needed to prove to the world that she wasn't a selfish, shallow person like her parents?

"No. We can't go back," she said, her voice barely above a whisper.

More than anything, Sam wanted to draw her against him, fold his arms around her and bury his face in her gossamer blond hair. But he knew that if he did, he wouldn't be able to stop there. He'd want to carry her to the tumbled bed behind them, peel the peach fabric away from her soft skin and bury himself in the warmth of her body.

Instead he dropped his hand away from her shoulders and tried to shove the image out of his mind. He couldn't make love to her even if she invited him to. His heart would be just as involved as his body. And he couldn't risk breaking it to pieces all over again.

"Well, I'd better get back to my room. Er, thanks for bandaging my hand."

Even though his words were drawled, she could hear a sense of urgency threaded through them, and knew he wanted to be gone from her and this room.

Her throat tight and achy, she continued to stare out the window as she spoke. "You're welcome, Sam. Good night."

As Sam left the room, he glanced at the bed and the photo album he'd tossed down on the rumpled covers. That was the real image of Olivia, he thought. Not the image he carried around in his heart, the image of Olivia as the wife of a farmer, the mother of his children. For the next couple of days he had to remember that.

Olivia had never had the opportunity to do much more than basic cooking. She felt proud of herself if she managed a plate of bacon and eggs, or a simple meat loaf. When it came to pie making she was in the kindergarten class and was quick to tell Ella so the next morning.

Ella chuckled. "I guess I've been baking pies for so long that it's hard for me to imagine anyone not knowing how."

Olivia stood next to the older woman as she watched her dump cinnamon and nutmeg into a bowl filled with pureed pumpkin. Across the counter from them Kathleen was busy pouring syrup into a frothy mixture of beaten eggs and sugar.

"Mother had me in the kitchen learning how to bake pies by the time I was eleven years old," Kathleen said to Olivia. "She said it was something every farmer's wife needed to know how to do."

Ella chuckled. "And then you ended up being a schoolteacher instead of a farmer's wife."

"Even so," Kathleen replied, "I'm still glad I know how to cook most anything."

"My mother would think it an insult if she had to get into the kitchen on Thanksgiving Day, or any day, for that matter," Olivia confessed.

"You're kidding!" Ella gasped.

"Not at all. Daddy always had everything catered in because he would give the cook the day off."

"How big of him," Kathleen said with a sarcastic grimace.

"Kathleen! You're speaking of Olivia's father!" Ella scolded.

Olivia shook her head, then shrugged philosophically. "She's only being honest."

"Lord, I can't imagine it," Ella said, shaking her head.

"Of course, my parents always invited guests over. But none of them were ever relatives, they were always business associates. Mother did the hostessing, but that was as far as it went." Olivia peered over Ella's shoulder as the older woman poured six raw eggs into the pumpkin mixture. "What are all the eggs for?"

Ella whipped the spoon vigorously through the orange-colored batter. "They sort of set everything together, but you also need a pinch or two of flour to make it all smooth."

"I could never learn how to do this," Olivia confessed.

"Sure you can," Kathleen spoke up. "Just get Mother's recipe and follow it to the letter."

Olivia laughed. "Sure. A pinch of this, a dash of that." She put her arm around Ella's waist and gave the older woman a gentle hug. "Ella, you cook like a chef who's had years of practice."

"I have, honey. Just about thirty-five years of it. Once Sam was born I had to learn how to cook. That kid ate like one of S.T.'s durocs."

At the mention of Sam, Olivia looked out the windows facing the barns. She hadn't seen him this morning. She'd been late coming down for breakfast and she supposed he'd already left the house to do some chores.

The weather was still misty and rainy, but inside the kitchen it was warm and bright. The radio was tuned to a country station and the rich smell of baking pies filled the air. Olivia was drinking it all in, enjoying every moment, because she knew that all too soon Thanksgiving would have come and gone. And she'd no longer have an excuse to stay with this giving family.

She was helping Kathleen place pecan halves on the dark, syrupy pie filling when the telephone rang. Ella quickly went to answer it.

Kathleen used the moment to question Olivia. "So tell me. How did things go last night?"

Olivia felt heat seep into her cheeks. "Last night?" Did Kathleen know that Sam had been in her bedroom last night?

Kathleen gave her friend an impatient look. "Yes. You know. While you were alone. Shelling pecans."

"Oh." Olivia sighed with relief, then said, "I guess you could say we were civil to one another."

"Is that all?" Kathleen looked disappointed. "Surely he had something to say. Didn't you feel any kind of sparks?"

Oh, she'd felt sparks, all right. But what good was that going to do? Sam didn't want her, at least not the way she wanted him. "Frankly, Sam has had a lot to say," she said.

Kathleen looked at her keenly. "Really? Like what?"

Olivia kept her eyes on the pecans she was placing across the pieshell. "Like how I hurt him by going to Africa."

"I suppose you did. But didn't he realize that you had studied and planned for four years to go over there? It was everything to you. Isn't it just like a man to think nothing else matters but himself and his own wants?" she muttered.

Olivia grimaced. "Back then I asked your brother to go with me. Did you know that?"

Kathleen shook her head ruefully. "I can see why you would. But I could have told you that Sam would never leave this farm. It's so much a part of him he'd only be half a man away from it."

"Yeah, well, I should have realized that. Instead, because he didn't want to go with me and help me with my cause, I accused him of not loving me."

Kathleen heaved a long sigh, then lifted one of the unbaked pies from the countertop. "And he accused you of not loving him because you wouldn't stay with him on the farm. What a mess you two were in."

Olivia crossed over to the oven and opened the door for Kathleen. "Well, I'm beginning to see that we didn't really have time enough to deal with our problems. Three weeks was long enough for us to fall in love, but it wasn't long enough to sort out how we might fit our lives together."

Kathleen bent over and carefully placed the pecan pie on the oven rack. "Well, you have the time now," she said.

Olivia didn't say anything. But she could have told her friend that all the time in the world wouldn't fix the problems standing between her and Sam.

Across the room, Ella placed the telephone back on its hook, then looked glumly at the two young women. "We might as well forget about making that orange salad," she said. "Nick isn't going to be able to make it home for Thanksgiving."

"Oh, was that Nick?" Kathleen asked eagerly. Then, before Ella could answer, she went on, "Why didn't you let me talk to him?"

Frowning, Ella crossed the room to join them. "He was in a hurry. Something about a lieutenant meeting him on the parade grounds in just a few minutes."

Kathleen tossed down the quilted gloves she'd used to put the pie in the oven. "The parade ground! Doesn't the army know it's nearly Thanksgiving?"

"I'm sure they do. But that doesn't mean they'll bring things to a grinding halt. Nick has some sort of duty Thanksgiving Day. There's no way he can come."

Kathleen was both disappointed and angry. "Well, that cuts it with me! I'm not sending that commanding officer of his a Christmas card this year."

Ella clucked her tongue. "We can't be selfish, Kathleen. There're other young men at Fort Sill who want to be home with their families, too. All of them can't be gone."

"But Mother, we haven't seen him in more than seven months!"

Olivia watched her friend slump onto a stool. "I'm sorry, Kathleen. I wished your brother could be here, too. I was looking forward to talking with him again."

Ella began to sniffle. "He'll probably get a slice of Spam and those horrible canned sweet potatoes for Thanksgiving dinner. I can't bear to think of it. Especially when I know how much he loves my candied sweet potatoes."

The door leading onto the back porch suddenly opened and Sam stepped inside. Apparently he'd been working out in the open this morning. The shoulders and arms of his coat were wet from the rain and so was the cap he'd pulled over his black hair.

He looked at the three women as he unbuttoned his coat. Olivia appeared uncomfortable, Kathleen angry and his mother weepy. "What the hell is going on?"

Chapter Eight

Kathleen went over and took her brother's arm. "Oh Sam, we got a call from Nick. He won't be able to be here for Thanksgiving."

He looked at his tearful mother, knowing how close she was to her other son. Nick and Ella had always had a special kind of relationship. Sam didn't resent the fact. Still, it bothered him to see her so stirred up over Nick's absence.

With Kathleen still hanging on his arm, he crossed the room to Ella's side. "Good Lord, Mom. It's not the end of the world just because Nick can't be here for Thanksgiving."

"That's easy for you to say, Samuel Taylor! You won't be eating Spam and canned potatoes like Nick will have to," she said fiercely, then began to weep all over again.

Frowning, Sam glanced at his sister, then back to his mother. "I really doubt he'll be eating Spam, Mom. The army does more than open a can to feed its troops."

Ella remained stubbornly silent, making Sam throw up his hands with frustration. "Mom, I'm disappointed, too. But we can't change the army's rules. We'll just have to look forward to seeing Nick at Christmas."

Ella grabbed a paper towel and blew her nose. "So he can call and say he can't make it again?"

"Mom, Nick has never missed Christmas," Kathleen said quickly.

"That's right," Sam added, feeling the need to defend his absent brother.

With a dismissive sniff, Ella went to the sink and began tossing pots and pans into the soapy water. Sam and Kathleen exchanged puzzled looks.

"You act as though Nick is deliberately staying away," Sam said to his mother.

"Sometimes I wonder," Ella muttered, then her shoulders suddenly sagged. "I don't know what I would have done if you'd decided to make your home somewhere else, like Nick did. I don't think I could have stood giving up both you boys."

Olivia's gaze went from mother to son with a heavy pang of guilt. How could she ever have thought she could separate Sam from his family? The ties were simply too strong. Even if he had agreed to go with her to Africa, she knew the bigger part of him would have remained here on the farm with his family. It wouldn't have worked, she realized. Sam would have wound up resenting her for making him give up all that was dear to him.

Sam laughed in an effort to lighten his mother's mood. "I'm just like Jake and Leo. You couldn't run me off with a big stick and a loud roar."

Glancing over her shoulder, Ella gave her son a smile, then turned and made a concentrated effort to dry her tears.

Sam was relieved. He couldn't deal with a woman's tears, including his mother's. He wasn't like Nick, who hugged and kissed and teased with an ease that came natural to him. He looked over at Olivia and wondered if she thought he was gruff and insensitive. Probably, he thought. But damn it all, it shouldn't matter to him what she thought. She'd be leaving soon. And he hated himself because that was all he could really think about.

He took off his cap and tossed it toward the kitchen table. "Where's the pecan pie? I want a piece."

Kathleen gave him a tired look. "Well, you're not getting any."

"And why not? Nick's not coming so that means there's going to be at least three or four extra pieces."

Before another word was said, Ella went over to the island work counter and picked up one of the pies she'd taken out of the oven earlier.

"We'll all have a piece of pie," she said brightly. "Olivia, would you make a pot of coffee, dear? You make such wonderful coffee."

Olivia smiled, glad to see the older woman was getting over her disappointment. "I'll be glad to make coffee. Just don't let Sam eat my piece of pie, too."

"I'll take the flyswatter to the table with me just in case he tries it," Ella said, her good humor quickly bubbling back.

As Olivia put the coffee makings together she wondered why she couldn't have been given a mother like Ella, one who would have invited her young daughter into a cozy kitchen, who would have praised her instead of always expecting more from her.

You make such wonderful coffee. It was a simple compliment, but it had lifted Olivia's heart. The Wescotts had never found anything to praise or compliment their daughter on. Instead they'd been constantly embarrassed because she wasn't like them. Being around this family made Olivia realize just how unloved she'd been while growing up.

Until she'd met Sam, she'd felt lacking, certain that no man could love her. How could they if her own parents didn't even love her? she had asked herself. But then she and Kathleen had become friends, and ultimately she'd fallen in love with Sam and he with her. Or so she'd wanted badly to believe. But in the end, he'd found her just as lacking as her parents had.

Olivia shook off the dismal thoughts to see the coffee was finished brewing, and the others were seated around the big wooden table. Quickly, she filled the cups she'd gathered on a lacquered tray, then crossed the room to join them.

Olivia could feel Sam's dark gaze on her as she passed the cups around the table. She wondered if he was thinking about last night and the things they'd talked about in her room. Or was he thinking ahead to when she would be gone?

"We've been giving Olivia cooking lessons," Kathleen told her brother.

Olivia took a seat next to Ella, which put her directly across from Sam. As she settled herself in the chair, she glanced over at him. One of his dark brows was curved in a mocking arch while, surprisingly, his brown eyes glinted with amusement. "You don't know how to cook?"

A blush spread across Olivia's face. "I can cook simple things," she said, suddenly feeling the need to defend herself.

His eyes narrowed, he continued to look at her as he brought the coffee cup to his lips. After he'd taken a careful sip, he said, "I thought you learned all about food in college."

"I did. The nutrition part of it. How and what our bodies require. That's nothing like cooking."

Leaning back in her chair, Kathleen very nearly glowered at her brother. "Don't tell me you're one of those men that think a woman should automatically know how to cook just because she's a woman.''

"I didn't say that," Sam said with an annoyed frown. "And why are you picking on me? Because Nick isn't going to get to come home you have to take it out on me?"

"Shut up and eat your pie," Kathleen muttered. "I wasn't picking on you. I was merely defending Olivia. Are you trying to hurt her feelings?"

"Hurt her feelings?" Sam repeated, obviously amazed by the suggestion. "I only asked her about her cooking!"

Kathleen sliced through her pie with a vicious whack. "Yes, well you did it in an arrogant, male way."

"How should I have done it, sis? Like this?" Turning to Olivia, he raised his voice several octaves. "You don't know how to cook, Olivia? My, my!"

He sounded so ridiculous that Olivia burst out laughing. Soon Kathleen was joining her.

Ella shook her head at the three of them. "You'd think four adults could manage to have a more meaningful conversation than this." She slanted one eye at her son. "What have you been doing this morning, anyway? I thought you went with S.T. to see about that fencing material."

"I've been cutting firewood down in the field by the river. I've got a load on the pickup now to take over to Allison's."

Ella nodded with approval as she chewed a mouthful of pie. "That's kind of you, son. I'm sure she'll appreciate it."

Over the past two days, Olivia had learned that Allison was a young woman living in the old Lee house across the road from the Gallagher farmhouse. Olivia hadn't met the other woman yet, but she was beginning to form an image from the bits and pieces of information Ella and Kathleen had given her.

"Heaven knows she needs it," Kathleen added. "I think the fireplace is the only heat she has in that old house."

"I would have loved for Allison to have spent Thanksgiving with us," Ella said over the rim of her coffee cup. "But she wants to spend it with her grandmother, who's in the nursing home. That's why I'm making a special food basket for her. I want her to have plenty to share with the other old folks."

"Well, I'm just wondering how you're going to get her to accept the pies and things you made for her," Kathleen put in. "If I know Allison, she'll tell you to give the food to someone who needs it more than she does."

"I'm sure she will," Ella responded. "But I'll convince her somehow."

"Allison is a lovely girl," Kathleen told Olivia. "I wish you could meet her before you go back home."

Olivia slowly sliced into the rich pecan pie. A lovely girl? And Sam was cutting wood for her? Maybe he wasn't as indifferent to women as Kathleen had led her to believe.

"I wish I could, too," Olivia murmured, but she only said so out of politeness. Actually, she wasn't too keen on meeting any woman that Sam might be fond of. Which was crazy. She had no right or reason to be even remotely jealous of Sam.

Olivia had only a bite of pie left on her plate when Sam scraped back his chair and swallowed the last of his coffee.

"Mom, the pie was delicious," he said, putting his cup down, then rising to his feet.

"I didn't make it. Kathleen did," Ella told him.

Grinning, Sam leaned over the table and pinched the end of his sister's nose. "You're a good cook, sis. Nick would salute you."

His sister gave him a whimsical smile. "Yeah, he probably would at that. Then he'd tell me some vulgar army joke."

Sam chuckled, knowing Kathleen was right. He turned to Olivia. "Would you like to go with me to unload Allison's wood?"

The invitation caused her mouth to virtually drop open. "I, uh, I'm helping your mother and sister deliver the food baskets to church," she said, while wondering what his motives could possibly be for wanting her to join him.

Shrugging as though it didn't matter to him if she went or not, he crossed to the door and reached for his still-damp cap and coat. "No problem. I just thought you might like a breath of fresh air."

"She does." Kathleen hurriedly spoke up, then, while Sam wasn't looking, made a silent motion for Olivia to get out of her chair. "We don't need her, do we, Mom?"

Ella, who was already stacking the dirty pie plates, shook her head. "I'd like for Olivia to get out and enjoy herself. I certainly didn't invite her to spend the holiday with us just so I could have extra help. Besides, Olivia has spent the past four years distributing food to the needy. I'm sure she'd like to do something else for a change."

"There will be plenty to help with when you get back," Kathleen insisted, obviously in an effort to urge Olivia to accept her brother's invitation. "We've got the silverware to polish, the floors to vacuum, laundry to wash. Shall I go on, or is that enough for you to help with?"

Olivia knew exactly what Kathleen was up to. She only wished she knew what was going on in Sam's head. "Okay, you've made your point," she said, then glanced over her shoulder at Sam. "Give me a minute and I'll meet you outside," she told him.

After grabbing her coat, Olivia hurried out the back door to see Sam waiting beside his truck. The long bed was loaded with pieces of split firewood. But what caught Olivia's attention were the two beautiful collies that had climbed atop the stacked wood.

"This must be Jake and Leo," she said, smiling up at the dogs.

Obviously knowing a friend when they saw one, the two dogs stood at the very edge of their high perch, their tails wagging furiously as they whined a greeting back down to her.

"It is," Sam replied. "And right now they're both mad at me for not letting them ride up in the cab. You should tell them it's your fault."

"I will not," she said, laughing. "You're the one who put them there, not me."

Sam quickly shushed her with a finger on his lips, even though he was relishing the sound of her laughter. "Don't say that where they can hear you. Don't you know that dogs understand about two thousand human words? They've probably already figured out what you said."

"You can make it up to them by giving them some turkey scraps tomorrow," Olivia assured him with another laugh.

The graveled drive leading away from the farmhouse and back to the county road was not much more than a quarter of a mile long. When they reached the cattle guard, Sam turned left. Olivia could see the old house sitting only a few hundred yards away, barely far enough for Sam to shift the truck into a higher gear.

"If you're too cold you can stay in the truck while I unload," Sam told her as he backed the vehicle up to the front porch.

Olivia shook her head. "I'll be fine," she told him. "After all, I came on this outing to get some fresh air."

Sam looked at her and knew he was on the verge of blushing. God, he hadn't done that since he was a teenager. But why should that be so surprising? he asked himself. Every time he looked at Olivia he felt young and foolish.

"I also asked you to come with me to make up for my arrogant male behavior."

"Which time?" she couldn't help but ask.

Sam saw amusement glinting in her blue eyes and knew she was teasing him. He was glad to see that she could still joke with him. "At the kitchen table," he said.

The heater in the truck was blowing full force, yet the motor hadn't been running long enough to make the truck warm. Olivia rubbed her mittened hands up and down her thighs in an effort to warm them. The sight had Sam wishing it was his hands sliding up her curvy thighs, warming her, inviting her to come into his arms.

"I've never seen your sister behave quite like that before. It surprises me," Olivia said after a moment. "Kathleen isn't one of those feminists who are always down on men."

Her voice penetrated his sensual thoughts, but it was a full moment before Sam could push them out of his mind and answer her. "Yeah, well, she—she had a bastard for a husband. I don't know why she loved him. But she did. Now that he's gone I don't know if she'll ever let herself get close to another man."

"I hope you're wrong. Kathleen is such a romantic at heart. She..." Embarrassed by what she'd been about to say, she broke off abruptly and glanced away from him.

"She what?" he prompted. "Has she mentioned some guy to you?"

Sighing, Olivia shook her head. "No, nothing like that. I was only going to say that she knows about you and me."

Sam's brown eyes narrowed dangerously. "What do you mean, you and me?"

Olivia threw up her hands and turned back to him. Her voice was tart when she answered. "There was a you and me once, you know. Or have you already forgotten? Do you plow your memories into the ground like you do a dead crop?"

"Oh, hell!"

Her nostrils flared with anger. "Oh, hell, what? What does that mean?"

"Nothing. I just wished—"

This time it was Sam who broke off and looked away from her.

Olivia felt her heart momentarily stop, then kick into high gear. "You wish. What do you wish, Sam?"

Her voice softened as she spoke his name. Its velvety sound called to him like nothing else could.

"I wish for a lot of things." Suddenly his face swung back around, his eyes leveled on hers. "I certainly wish Kathleen didn't know how stupid you and I once were!"

Outrage widened Olivia's blue eyes. "Oh, so we were stupid to fall in love. Well, I can say one thing, Sam. It was certainly stupid on my part. Especially to think that you *could* really love me."

"I did love you!"

Her eyes darkened to an angry blue blaze. "You certainly had a peculiar way of showing it. Telling me you'd never speak to me again if I went to Africa!"

Had he really said that? Yes, he probably had. He'd been so hurt, so desperate to change her mind that he'd lashed out like a wounded lion, saying anything and everything to defend his pride.

"I wanted you to stay here, with me! Can't you understand that? Maybe it was selfish of me. But I needed you too, Olivia. It may not have been the same way some hungry child living halfway around the world needed you, but I did need you."

And Olivia had needed him, she'd just been too blind to see it. She rubbed her hands over her face, then took a long, calming breath. "I didn't think you were selfish. Not really," she murmured, the anger suddenly draining out of her. "I was very hurt that you wouldn't come with me. I thought..." Her eyes brimmed with tears. She shook her head and did her best to laugh them off, but the sound came out choked. "I thought if you really loved me you would come after me."

"To Africa?"

From the shocked look on his face, she could see that the thought had never entered his mind. "Yes. To Africa. Men have gone to greater lengths than that to go after the women they love."

Sam's head swung back and forth as though he couldn't believe what she was saying. "And what good would it have done, Olivia, if I'd gone to Africa to fetch you? You and I both know you would have refused to come with me. You had a dream to live. And it was much more important to you than being my wife!"

Kathleen was right—only a man could make a woman feel this much pain and anger at the same time. "You think you know so much about me, Sam Gallagher. But you don't know diddly squat!"

Blindly, Olivia reached for the door handle to let herself out of the truck. Yet before she could get a hold on it, Sam grabbed her shoulders from behind and twisted her around to face him.

"What are you trying to say now?" he said through gritted teeth.

Olivia's face was paper white with anger as she relived in her mind those first few months after she'd arrived in Ethiopia.

"It means you don't know what I was feeling! You don't know how shattered and hurt I was over your rejection. It means you'll never know how alone and scared I was because you didn't want me in your life. All I had was me. So don't talk to me about what I needed or didn't need, because you didn't know! What's more, you didn't want to know!"

As the last of her words died away, something sparked in Sam's eyes, but Olivia was too angry to really see it for what it was. She wanted away from him. Away from his ridicule and indifference.

Twisting out of his grasp, Olivia reached for the door handle. This time she managed to release the latch and the door swung open.

Cursing audibly, Sam lunged across her lap and grabbed the door. "Damn it, woman! I didn't bring you out here to fight with you."

He slammed the door shut, then pulled away from her. Olivia made a point of looking at him.

"Why did you bring me out here, Sam?"

His answer was a glare that fueled Olivia's temper all over again.

"Well, I'm waiting," she went on. "Why did you? So you could seduce me into making love with you, then tell me I made you do it?"

"Maybe I did," he growled, his eyes boring into hers.

Olivia saw a fire ignite in his eyes and knew in the back of her mind that she'd goaded him too far. But a part of her had wanted to push him to the same desperate place he'd put her in four years ago.

"Maybe I brought you out here to show you that you still want me."

That was ludicrous, she thought wildly. She already knew she wanted him. He just didn't know it. And she wasn't about to let him know it. He would only use the knowledge to hurt her, to rub her pride in the dirt all over again.

"What would that prove?" she asked, her voice losing some of its earlier confidence.

His mouth crooked into a mocking sneer. "I don't know. Maybe we should find out."

Before Olivia could respond to that, he pulled her into his arms. She struggled momentarily, but realized it was futile as his hand anchored itself on her nape.

The moment his lips came down on hers, Sam's anger vanished like mist in the wind. The sweet taste of her humbled him, and with an odd sense of helplessness, he knew he would always want this woman. No matter how far away from him she went, she would be like a thorn in his heart.

Olivia braced herself against the coming onslaught, but it never happened. Instead of taking savage possession, his lips brushed against hers, teasing, testing, asking.

Like a delicate blossom, her lips parted, unconsciously inviting him to taste their warmth. She was like a fine fruity wine, Sam decided, one that brought a tanginess to his tongue, a headiness to his senses. And once he became addicted to the flavor, he knew he would never be able to let her go.

The stark reality of that thought had Sam jerking away from her so abruptly his head spun. Olivia could only stare at him, her breast heaving, her hands trembling. What was he doing to her, she wondered desperately. Why was he trying to hurt her this way?

Sometime during the embrace Sam's cap had fallen from his head. He raked his fingers through his hair, then reached for the cap. From the corner of his eye he could see Olivia's face. It had a pale, wounded look. Her eyes were darkly accusing, her lips trembling.

God, he hadn't meant for any of this to happen, he thought miserably. He didn't know why he couldn't be alone with her for more than five minutes without things escalating into all-out warfare between them.

"Olivia, I—"

"I don't want to hear it!" she said, furiously cutting him off. "And I don't want your Thanksgiving kisses, either! As far as I'm concerned they're too little, too late!"

Grabbing for the door, she wrenched it open, then slid to the ground. Sam's mouth snapped shut, then fell open again.

"Where are you going?" he demanded.

"Back to the house. You can go unload your girlfriend's wood without me."

She slammed the door shut and took off walking toward the road with Jake and Leo close at her heels. Quickly, Sam slid across the seat and jerked the door open again.

"Allison is not my girlfriend!" he yelled after her.

She hesitated long enough to glance back over her shoulder at him. "Then all I can say is, lucky girl!"

Olivia didn't know later how she'd managed to walk into the house and pretend that everything was fine. She'd told Ella and Kathleen she'd walked to give herself some much-needed exercise. The two women hadn't questioned her and she'd breathed a sigh of relief that they'd believed her. But she'd spent the rest of the day wondering how she was going to handle herself once Sam came back to the house.

Thankfully, he didn't show up until suppertime, and the hustle and bustle of getting things ready for the meal provided her with a reason to ignore him.

But now that he was sitting directly across from her at the table, she didn't know how much longer she could pretend to be normal. She could feel his dark eyes sliding over her in ways she couldn't understand. He seemed to be asking her to look at him, but the moment she did, his gaze would falter and turn away.

"I sure do hate that Nick isn't going to make it tomorrow," S.T. said. "I'd like to see my other son once in a while. The boy is getting to be a stranger around here."

Ella, who was ladling pinto beans into a soup bowl, said, "The army is his family now. Not us, S.T." She handed him the beans, then reached for another bowl.

"Well, that doesn't mean I have to like it," S.T. insisted with a snort.

Olivia crumbled corn bread into her beans as she looked down the table at Sam's father. "Are you going to stay in Texas for Thanksgiving next year, S.T.?"

The big man shook his head. "I doubt it, honey. The farm will always be home and I want to be home on Thanksgiving. Where are you going to be? Over there in Africa?"

Olivia shrugged and did her best to laugh. "You never know about me, S.T. You might find me anywhere."

He laughed along with her. "Well, I know one thing. You've got a standing invitation to spend Thanksgiving at the Gallagher house."

S.T.'s kind words would have meant so much more if she'd known that Sam echoed his father's feelings. As it was, she couldn't bear to think of coming back here next year or any other year for Thanksgiving.

"It would be lovely if all of us could be together like this next year," Kathleen said, her glance moving from Sam to Olivia and back again. "With Nick, too, naturally."

Beneath her lowered lashes, Olivia could see a tight grimace cross Sam's face, and she felt her heart crack a little bit more.

"That's what makes holidays so special," Ella spoke up. "Everybody being together, loving one another, laughing, eating."

"And eating again," S.T. added with humorous emphasis.

"You're right, Daddy," Kathleen said happily. "And who knows more about eating than a Gallagher?"

Olivia glanced once again at Sam, but he refused to look her way. It was as if he were trying to deliberately exclude her from his family and his life. The idea twisted something deep within her heart.

"We know how to raise a crop and we know how to eat it," Sam added in his deep voice. "I'm thankful I was born a farmer."

S.T. looked affectionately down the table at his strong, handsome son. "I'm thankful you were born a farmer, too, son. Otherwise I wouldn't be able to retire and leave this old place in your capable hands. And that would mean come the end of this winter I couldn't go to Texas and fish every day with my brother."

Sam smiled modestly at his father's praise and S.T. lifted his bowl of beans as if in a toast.

"So here's to beans and corn bread on Thanksgiving Eve. I want the good Lord to know I'm just as thankful for them as I will be for that fat turkey we carve tomorrow."

"Here, here!" Ella seconded.

"Amen," Kathleen added.

Olivia looked around the table and knew she should be feeling thankful and happy, too. Instead, she realized she'd never felt more alone in her life. She wasn't a part of this loving family. She never would be.

After supper, Sam went to the den to work at his desk. In the morning's mail, he'd received a letter from the University of Arkansas. The agricultural department was constantly doing scientific research on crops, fertilizers, insecticides—anything that would make farming more efficient and profitable. Normally Sam looked forward to reading about the university's findings. In many instances he'd applied some of the information to his own crops. But tonight his thoughts drifted after only two or three lines.

With a sigh of frustration, he tossed the letter to one side, then rubbed a hand over his face. He might as well face the fact, he told himself. Olivia was driving him crazy. That's all there was to it. He wished like hell Nick was here. His younger brother was much more experienced at dealing with women than Sam was. Maybe Nick could tell him something to get this jumbled mess straightened out in his head.

That afternoon at the Lee house, when Olivia had walked away, Sam had been more stunned than anything. Yet by the time he'd unloaded the wood, he'd regretted the impulsive things he'd said to her. It was like there was a demon inside him, pushing him to hurt not only her, but himself, too.

S.T. entered the den and took up his usual place in an oversize recliner. His father loved Westerns and usually read one every night.

Sam watched his father switch on the floor lamp by his chair, then open the paperback book on his lap. There was no man he admired more in the world than Samuel Taylor Gallagher, his father. But Sam was old enough and wise enough to know that S.T. was not just a father. He was also a man who'd experienced the same sort of troubles that other men had faced.

"Dad?"

"Hmm?"

"What was it like when you and Mom fell in love?"

The question had the older man peering over the rim of his glasses at his son.

"What do you mean?"

Sam shrugged, embarrassed for asking the question in the first place. "I just mean—well, was your romance smooth sailing? Did everything just fall into place like you wanted it to?"

S.T. chuckled heartily. "Now how do you think I could have had smooth sailing while romancing a woman like your mother? She was a wildcat back in those days. I had to take things slow and tread lightly."

"You have a good marriage now," Sam countered.

"'Course we do. But your mother has mellowed with age. And so have I," he admitted with a wry grin.

"So it was worth all the ups and downs you went through to get her?" Sam asked.

S.T. pulled the eyeglasses from his face and rubbed the bridge of his nose. "Hell, son, without your mother, I wouldn't be anything." He waved the glasses about the room around them. "Sure, I have a farm, money in the bank and the good health to enjoy it. But none of that is like having a woman by your side. Nothing is like that."

Sam was beginning to see what his father meant. Tomorrow on Thanksgiving Day he would have a lot to be thankful for. But he knew all of it would mean so much more if he had Olivia by his side, sharing his life and his home.

His life. His home. If Olivia could hear his thoughts she would think him selfish. She'd dedicated her life to helping others. How could he ask her to give up her work a second time? Things hadn't really changed as far as he could see. Except that this time he knew how truly genuine her reasons were for going to Africa. And knowing that, he couldn't ask her to sacrifice her dreams just for him. Even if by some miracle she did agree to stay, she would more than likely wind up resenting the hell out of him.

Wearily, Sam scrubbed his face with his hands, while across the room his father went back to his Western. However, only a few moments passed before S.T. lowered the book and said, "One of these days, Sam, you and Nick are each going to find some woman you know you can't live without. And being men, you'll probably think you'll have a choice in the matter. But you won't have a choice. Not really. You'll have to have her, one way or the other."

Sam looked at his father and knew he didn't have the heart to tell the older man that he'd found that woman four years ago, but he'd lost her.

Chapter Nine

Olivia was grateful there were still more preparations to be done for Thanksgiving dinner. It gave her an excuse to stay in the kitchen and away from Sam. The less she saw of him, the better off she knew she would be. She couldn't understand his hot-and-cold attitude, any more than she could understand why she couldn't stop loving him.

"Mother, what time are you going to put the turkey in the oven? Do I need to get up early to help you?" Kathleen asked.

"There's no need for you to get up, too," Ella answered. "I can manage. I've already put him in the roasting pan, so he's ready to go."

Olivia and Kathleen were crumbling corn bread, biscuits and bread slices into a galvanized wash pan. As Olivia studied the growing mound of bread, she wondered how Ella expected five adults to eat so much stuffing.

"Don't you think half of this pan will be enough?" Olivia asked. "This should make tons of dressing."

"I want to have plenty," Ella assured her. "There are always friends dropping in before the day is over and they all expect to be fed."

Kathleen laughed. "I think it's more like you expect them to eat."

Ella smiled guiltily at her daughter. "I told Fred and Lillian to come by. And of course I told Allison to drop in after she takes her grandmother back to the nursing home. Who knows who else might show up?"

"And Mother would be very disappointed if they didn't," Kathleen told Olivia.

"Of course I would," Ella said as she put the finishing touches on a mincemeat pie. "Thanksgiving is a time for friends to gather as well as families."

Olivia watched the older woman work meticulously over the pie and wondered what next Thanksgiving would be like for herself. Where would she be? Her African home was gone and she certainly couldn't come back here. Maybe with her parents? That idea was hardly worth considering. She'd rather spend the day alone in her apartment than spend it socializing with business people she'd never met before.

It was nearly bedtime before the three women decided they had everything done that needed to be. Ella suggested they go into the den and have a glass of much-deserved wine before they all went to bed.

Olivia would have preferred to go straight to her room and avoid the chance of an encounter with Sam. But she knew that was foolish. If Sam really wanted to say anything else to her, he would have probably already cornered her. Her fears had been unwarranted. Sam was nowhere in sight. Neither was S.T.

"Poor men," Ella said as she curled up in a stuffed rocking chair. "The two of them worked so hard getting ready for tomorrow I guess they had to go to bed early."

Kathleen laughed, and Olivia smiled as she took a small sip from the glass of wine Ella had given her.

"Mother, you know Daddy will need to be rested to watch the football games," Kathleen said jokingly. "He puts all of himself into every play."

"What about Sam—does he like football?" Olivia asked, realizing there were many things about him she didn't know. Those three weeks she'd spent here at the farm had been long enough to fall in love, long enough to change the course of her life, but not long enough to learn all those little things about the man she would like to know.

"Sam likes any sport that involves a ball of some sort," Ella answered.

"He and Nick both played football in high school," Kathleen told Olivia. "He played defensive end and Nick played running back. Of course, there were too many years' age difference for them to play on the same team."

"Oh Lord, do I ever remember those days," Ella said fondly. "All those games where we had to sit huddled beneath blankets or holding umbrellas over our heads."

Kathleen looked at Olivia and smiled. "We went to a few of those ourselves in our college days, didn't we?"

Olivia nodded as she recalled that brighter time in her life. It seemed like such a long time ago since she'd been that happy and carefree. She'd had her whole life planned out before her, and she'd been so confident that it would all happen just the way she wanted it to.

She'd been young and naive then, she realized now. But the hardship of Africa plus the heartache of losing Sam had caused her to grow up very quickly. Looking back, it was easy to see the many wrong turns she'd taken in her life. Yet it wasn't so easy to know how to overcome those mistakes and try to build her future again.

A few minutes later Ella and Kathleen decided to retire for the night. Olivia wished them good-night, then refilled her wineglass and carried it over to the fireplace.

She hoped the extra bit of alcohol would lull her to sleep once she went up to her bedroom. The last thing she wanted to do was spend another night thinking of Sam lying just across the hall from her.

Out in the breezeway, Sam headed toward the staircase, then paused when he spotted a dim light coming from the den. His first instinct was to ignore it. His father was more than likely still reading. But there had been a fire in the fireplace earlier, he suddenly remembered. It wouldn't hurt to check and see if the safety doors on it were closed. If a burning log rolled out onto the floor, it would be only a matter of minutes before everything went up in blazes.

The moment Sam stepped into the room, he spotted Olivia sitting on the carpet in front of the fireplace. Her legs were drawn up against her chest, her chin resting on her knees. A wineglass was cradled between her hands, where she'd linked them together at her ankles.

Her fine blond hair hung loose and partially covered her face, but he could see that she was gazing pensively into the fire. The light of the flames bathed her features and hair with a soft, rosy glow. She was incredibly beautiful and he felt himself being drawn into the room, even though he knew he should turn and leave before she spotted him.

Olivia sensed more than heard Sam enter the room. When he came to a halt only a foot or two away from her, she turned her head to look at him.

Noticing he was wearing a coat and cap, she asked, "Have you been outside?"

Nodding, Sam reached up and pulled the cap from his head. Olivia watched his black hair slide with abandon across his forehead.

"Down at the barn checking on the hogs. I wanted to make sure they had enough dry bedding to keep them warm."

"I didn't realize hogs needed that much sheltering from the cold," she admitted.

"As far as I'm concerned they do. Animals thrive on good care and attention." His eyes flicked over her up-turned face. "What are you doing still up?"

Her heart began a rapid thud against her ribs. Was he thinking she'd been waiting up for him? "Just unwinding and enjoying the fire."

She wanted to enjoy those simple things as much as she could before she headed back to Africa, he thought wearily. How was he ever going to say goodbye? How was he going to watch her leave, knowing she'd be out of his life for good?

Olivia watched him unbutton his coat, then toss it over the arm of a nearby rocking chair. Beneath it he was wearing an old flannel shirt that had been washed so many times the red plaid had faded to a melon pink. On one elbow, the worn threads had split to show a patch of white thermal underwear. Yet he wore the garments with the same flair of authority as a well-suited stockbroker.

As he eased down beside Olivia on the carpet, she suddenly knew why. Sam was sure of who he was and where he belonged. He was proud of his family heritage and proud of the fact that he was carrying it on in the same tradition. He'd probably never regretted any choice he'd made in his life.

Olivia wished she could say the same for herself. But she couldn't. Funny, she thought, how clearly she could see things now. Marrying Sam and living with him here on the farm would have made her happy. It was the choice she'd really wanted to make. But at the time he'd proposed to her, she'd been mixed up with ambition, calling and a sense of duty that told her that she had to carry through with her previous plans.

"I'm glad you haven't gone to bed," he said.

Olivia couldn't hide her surprise, or her wariness. "Oh? Why is that? So you can tell me I acted like an idiot this afternoon?"

Grimacing, he reached for the glass in her hands, and she released it to him. There was something intimate, even sensual about sharing her glass with him, she realized as she watched him drink the last of the wine. The idea of his lips touching the same spot as hers sent a wave of unbidden desire coursing through her.

Sam carefully set the glass aside, then turned back to her. Olivia's eyes went straight to his lips as she imagined what it would be like if he would take her into his arms and kiss her. Not to punish or degrade her, but to simply make love to her.

"No," he said. "To tell you that *I* acted like one. I'm sorry."

She drew in a long, quivering breath. He was sorry? She couldn't believe what she was hearing. "There's no need for you to say you're sorry, Sam. You were only saying what you felt. And I don't think a person should be sorry for telling the truth—as he sees it." Even if the truth hurts, her heart silently added.

He gave her a long, searching glance, then turned toward the fire. "Let's face it, Olivia. I've been a real bastard these past three days." He let out a heavy sigh, then turned his gaze back to hers. "I guess I..." He stopped and shook his head, then started over again. "When I first saw you, all I could think about was making you hurt, the way you had hurt me. I know you didn't come here for that. You came her to see Kathleen and my parents."

She studied his face, wondering if she might be able to read more from it than she could his words. But the longer her eyes explored him, the less she thought of his words. He was so close and his strong dark features were so appealing. She wanted him, she realized, probably more than she ever had in her life.

"What makes you think I didn't come here to see you, too?" she asked softly.

Her question obviously surprised him. His brows lifted, his lips parted.

"Because if you'd wanted to see me, you would have come back a long time ago," he reasoned.

Olivia couldn't stop herself from moving close to him and touching the side of his face. As she slid her palm along the length of his jaw, the faint stubble of his beard acted as a sweet abrasion against her skin. "I wish I had come back a long time ago, Sam. I truly do."

Sam didn't know which shocked him more, the feel of her touching his face, or the conviction he heard in her softly spoken words.

"Do you really expect me to believe that, Olivia?"

Her hand slid from his cheek to curve gently over his forearm. "No. I guess I don't," she said softly. "Looking back, I can see that I expected too much from you. I expected you to know how I felt about becoming a relief worker, about the way I felt about my parents. I expected you to leave your home and your family behind. Then I expected and hoped you'd come after me." The memories were suddenly assaulting her, forcing her to stop and swallow. "When—when you didn't come after me, I hoped I could make it up to you with letters. God, it's no wonder you didn't read them. I guess I must have seemed pretty selfish and childish back then."

As Sam looked into her eyes he felt a pang of longing so intense he didn't think he could bear it. He caught her hand and folded it between his. "Olivia, those letters—I was so angry with you I couldn't bring myself to read them. But

I'm asking you now, would it have made a difference if I had read them?''

Olivia couldn't look at him as she thought about those letters, still sealed as they were when she'd mailed them, and packed in a chest at her apartment. She wished she had them with her. She'd give them to him to read, and maybe then he could answer that question for himself. But since they weren't with her, he would more than likely never read them. And maybe it was better that way, she thought.

"I don't know, Sam," she murmured. "Four years ago, we both wanted different things in our lives. I don't want to be bitter about that anymore. I wish you wouldn't be, either."

She moved her hand away from his arm and Sam instantly felt the disconnection. He wanted her to touch him again, and keep on touching him. He wanted to draw her into his arms, kiss her lips, bury his face in her hair, taste the sweet softness of her skin. Was he crazy to want such things? Was he crazy to think that they could somehow erase the past and start over?

"I'm not . . . bitter anymore, Olivia." And he wasn't, he realized. His heart had moved beyond the bitterness and on to the future. But how could Olivia be a part of his future if she was going back to Africa in a few weeks?

The sincerity in Sam's voice went straight to Olivia's heart. Suddenly, she wanted to throw herself into his arms, tell him how much she loved him. She wanted to hear him say that he could forgive her, that she really did mean something to him after all. But he didn't want that. He'd proved that this afternoon when he'd jerked away from their kiss as if it had soiled him.

Silent moments passed and he didn't say anything else. Olivia realized he was waiting for her to answer his earlier question about the letters. She looked into the fire and reluctantly began to speak.

"After I was in Africa a few weeks, I realized I'd made a bad mistake, Sam. But I didn't know what to do about it. All I could think about was you. I was miserable without you, and I hated myself for being so headstrong and determined to have things my way. I thought if I wrote to you and explained . . ."

Afraid that she wouldn't continue, Sam leaned over and placed a finger under her chin. Slowly, he drew her face up to his. "Explain what, Olivia? Tell me. I want to know." He needed to know!

Olivia tried her best to smile at him, to make him believe that her feelings were all in the past. But her lips felt as stiff and frozen as her heart. "I tried to tell you how much I loved you. That I knew I'd made the wrong choice and that I wanted to come home and be your wife—if you still wanted me."

Sam felt as if a fist had been rammed into his midsection. He couldn't speak. He wasn't even sure that he could breathe. He felt sick with regret. Sick with the utter loss of it all.

He looked across the dimly lit room. But he wasn't seeing the familiar furnishings where his family always gathered in the evening. His mind was a kaleidoscope of past scenes playing out in his mind. Scenes of Olivia pleading with him, kissing him, arguing with him. Scenes of Olivia with tears on her face as she'd said her last goodbye to him.

Determined to go on, Olivia cleared her throat and started again. "When I received my letter back unopened, I thought there had been a mix-up in the mail. The international post can be a pain sometimes. So I wrote another. But when that letter came back also, I realized that you didn't want to hear from me."

She shrugged in an effort to appear as nonchalant as she could even though her heart was aching. "I wrote to you a few more times after that. I don't know why it took me so long to accept that you'd gone on with your life and didn't want me in it. Some of my Wescott stubbornness, I suppose.''

Dear God, she must have felt like he was slapping her in the face each time he'd sent one of those letters back to her. She'd been trying to tell him that she loved him. And he'd been too full of hurt pride to listen.

Sensing that Olivia was no longer by his side, he looked around to see she'd gotten to her feet. He rose to stand beside her. As their eyes met she gave him a tremulous little smile. One that said "it's all over and done with, I've put you in the past so you won't be bothered with me anymore.''

Sam didn't know if he could possibly hurt more than he did at this moment. "I didn't know, Olivia.''

"Well, I guess back then there was a lot that neither of us knew about each other, or about ourselves,'' she said quietly.

Sam knew that he had loved her then, and he knew he loved her now. What would she think if he told her how he really felt? Would she even believe him after the hateful way he'd treated her these past days?

"You know, I used to think that part of the reason you left was because you didn't like the farm. That you didn't want to be a farmer's wife.''

Had he really believed that? God, she could imagine how that must have hurt his pride. "It wasn't like that at all, Sam.'' She made a helpless gesture with her hands. "I didn't know that much about farming then. But I'd hoped . . .''

The firelight flickered over her ivory skin as Sam studied her face and waited for her to continue. She was so soft and warm, so beautiful. He wanted to make love to her. He wanted to make her so much a part of him that she would never want to leave again.

"You'd hoped what?" he prompted, his husky voice echoing the sensual thoughts in his head.

Olivia didn't want to tell him. She wanted to bring this whole conversation to an end. It hurt too much to think about the wasted years standing between them. But she knew that Sam would never allow her to stop here.

Sighing despondently, she closed her eyes. "I hoped that if you asked me to come back to you, I could learn all about farm living. I think you know me well enough, Sam, to know that I never wanted to be just an adornment. I wanted this place to be my home. I wanted to be a real working partner."

Her words ripped him apart with frustration and regret. Muttering an oath, he thrust his fingers through his hair and lifted his face to the ceiling. "I wanted this place to be your home, too, Olivia."

His voice sounded so weary that a hollow ache began to creep through her, until she felt tears burn her throat and threaten to fill her eyes.

Desperate not to let him see how shaken she was, she bent and picked up the empty wineglass, then carried it across to a low coffee table.

As Sam watched her move across the room, everything inside of him wanted to carry her upstairs to his bed and keep her there until she forgot all about Africa and its starving people. He wanted to show her how much he was starving for her love. "Does Africa still mean so much to you, Olivia?"

Wary now, she kept her back to him. "Why do you ask?"

He moved toward her. "It's a simple question, Olivia. Does going back to Africa mean as much to you now as it did four years ago?"

She bent her head, then groaned and covered her face with her hands. "I don't want to talk about it, Sam."

"Why?"

The sound of his voice warned her that he was only inches away. Just knowing he was that near made Olivia tremble inside and out. "Because it hurts. Because it's not like you think—"

He moved a step closer and placed his hands on her shoulders. For a moment he simply stood there, savoring the warmth of her, the soft, womanly scent of her. "Do you have to go back there to be happy, Olivia?" he finally asked. "There're plenty of needy people here in Arkansas. There are all sorts of missions and shelters in Fort Smith and Van Buren that are crying for someone like you to help them."

Oh God, why was he doing this to her? she wondered. Why was he making her feel, making her think about all the things she'd lost? "Oh, yeah. Olivia Wescott could really help."

Her voice was low, but he didn't miss the self-mockery in it. Her attitude both angered and puzzled him, and he gave her shoulders a little shake. "Why not? You've spent the past four years helping save lives. Don't tell me you don't know how to deal with the hungry, the poor, the homeless."

Some of the protective walls she'd built around her came crashing down and a reckless feeling took over. She whirled around to face him. "You don't know what you're saying to me, Sam! You don't know what went on in Ethiopia. I've spent the past four years watching people die! Do you have any idea what that has done to me? Do you know how useless and empty that makes me feel?"

Beneath his hands, he could feel her trembling. The idea that she could be in that much anguish tore at him. Instinctively, he started to pull her into his arms, but she held herself away from him and shook her head vehemently.

"Olivia, why—"

"I'm used up, Sam. I'm not going back to Africa. I can't go back. What little I have left of myself would fall apart if

I went," she said flatly. "So go ahead. Rub it in. Tell me how you were right all along."

Sam stared at her as though she'd just whopped him over the head, then anger sparked in his brown eyes. "Rub it in? Damn it all, Olivia! You've been leading me to think—no, not just me, but my whole family—that you were going back to Ethiopia. What in hell did you hope to accomplish by not telling the truth?"

"I wasn't trying to accomplish anything. I was trying to avoid—this!" She gritted her teeth and glared back at him.

"This? What—"

"Don't you know? I didn't want to admit to you that I had failed at my job—" her voice broke, forcing her to swallow before she could continue "—because I knew you'd be smug about it. You warned me not to go and I wouldn't listen to you."

Sam looked as though she'd slapped him. "Do you think I'm that much of a bastard?"

Olivia had thought so two days ago when she'd first arrived. Now she wasn't so sure. Maybe he didn't want to intentionally hurt her. But he was hurting her just the same. "I don't know."

Before he could say more, Olivia jerked loose from his hold and quickly stepped around him. Yet she'd barely made it halfway across the room when Sam caught hold of her upper arm and tugged her back to him.

"Why can't you be honest with me, Olivia? We both know what you're really trying to avoid," he said fiercely.

The dark passion on his face stunned her. Was it hate? Was it love? What did he want from her? she wondered wildly. "I don't know what you're talking about."

"Oh, yes, you do," he hissed, then jerked her into his arms. "You don't want to have to deal with the way I make you feel."

Olivia's heart began to thud crazily as his hands caught both sides of her face. "I . . . you don't make me feel anything. I can't feel anything. Not anymore."

"You know that's not true. At this very moment I can feel the pulse in your neck hammering away. And if I kissed you . . ."

He didn't go on. Olivia probably wouldn't have heard the words even if he had. All she could do was feel as he drew her face upward and covered her mouth with his.

Heat soared through Olivia's body as his lips took control, his tongue parted her teeth. Groaning, she leaned into him, then latched her arms around his neck as she gave herself up to the hot, blinding kiss.

Long minutes later Sam forced himself to lift his head. Desire had turned his eyes dark and heavy lidded. Olivia gazed up at him, wanting more than anything to pull his head back down to hers.

"Haven't you guessed by now that I still want you, Olivia?" he murmured against her lips.

He still wanted her. Oh yes, Olivia could feel how he wanted her. She was beginning to wonder if that was all Sam had ever felt for her—just a hot desire that had now rekindled itself.

Suddenly she knew she had to get out of his arms and away from him. She couldn't think when his touch, his kiss was making her drunk, making her vulnerable to everything he was saying.

"I can't deal with this now, Sam," she said as she slowly and deliberately drew away from his embrace. "Please—let me go."

The last thing Sam wanted to do was let her go. But he would. Because this time, he promised himself, it would be for only a little while.

As she was turning away, his hand caught her fingers and for a moment he held on to them tightly.

"Whatever you might think, Olivia, I'm not glad that you failed at your job. I'm not glad that you had to watch people die or that it tore you apart. But I will say I'm damn glad you're not going back. So make what you will of that."

Olivia couldn't bring herself to look at him. And even if she could she wouldn't have seen him for the tears filling her eyes and spilling onto her cheeks.

"Good night, Sam," she whispered.

Her fingers slipped from his and she fled the room. It was all Sam could do to stand there and let her go.

Chapter Ten

Thanksgiving morning, Sam thought as he looked out his bedroom window at the sun rising over the fields. It had always been one of his favorite days of the year, a holiday that symbolized everything a farmer worked for and held dear to his heart.

For as many Thanksgivings as he could remember, Sam had gotten up to the smell of turkey roasting in the oven. And because she always wanted everybody to be hungry for the big dinner, Ella would fix only toast and coffee for breakfast.

Sam knew when he went downstairs he would find everything the same—the smells, the warmth of the kitchen, the rows of pies lining the window seat. The toast and coffee. S.T. would more than likely be standing at Ella's shoulder, dipping his finger in a dish of food when her head was turned, or kissing her cheek when it wasn't.

Yes, it would all be the same, he thought. Except this time Olivia would be there. She'd be sitting at the breakfast table with her platinum hair and sad blue eyes.

He'd lain awake most of the night thinking about her. Thinking about them. The fact that she wasn't going back to Africa had turned everything around in his mind. But he was still no closer to understanding her than before.

Sam realized that her ordeal in Africa had drained her emotionally. No doubt dealing with famine and death would drain even the strongest person. But he knew there was a deep-rooted need in her to help others. Right now she might think she didn't have anything of herself left to give, but he somehow had to make her see that she was wrong. And if she could see that, then maybe she could also see that they belonged together.

Olivia stood back from the vanity mirror and eyed herself from several different angles. She'd decided to dress this morning in a soft amber-colored dress, cut straight and simple with long sleeves and a scooped neckline.

It looked passable, she supposed, but she wanted to look more than passable. She wanted to look as pretty as she could. She was going to smile and be happy today no matter what.

A light knock sounded on the bedroom door. Olivia went to open it and found Kathleen standing on the other side, an excited smile on her face.

"Happy Thanksgiving," she said.

Olivia pushed the door wider so that Kathleen could enter the room. "Happy Thanksgiving to you. What are you doing up so early?

Kathleen laughed as though the question was absurd. "What are *you* doing up so early?"

Olivia made a helpless gesture with her hand before she ran it through her tousled hair. "I'm just like a child when it comes to special holidays. And it's been so long since I've gotten to celebrate one properly."

Kathleen sank down on the end of the bed and gracefully crossed her long legs. "Well, you certainly look beautiful in that dress. You're going to make me look dowdy."

Olivia eyed the deep blue pleated skirt and matching sweater covering Kathleen's tall, shapely figure.

"You, dowdy? That'll be the day. I'd kill for your thick hair. And you'll never know what it's like to be five foot two."

Kathleen laughed. "You make five foot two look like the height every woman should be." She rose from the bed and pushed Olivia down onto the bench in front of the vanity. "Here, let me brush your hair for you."

Olivia handed the hairbrush to Kathleen. "I'm sure Ella is already in the kitchen, isn't she?"

Kathleen nodded as she fluffed Olivia's blond hair with the brush. "Actually, she's in the den drinking coffee with Daddy. He's waiting for Macy's Thanksgiving Day parade to come on TV."

An American tradition, Olivia thought with fond remembrance. It reminded her just how many things she'd missed since she'd been out of the country, and how glad she was to be back.

"Gosh, it's been a long time since I've seen one of those. Do they still have a giant Mickey Mouse floating up over the streets?"

"We'll watch and see," Kathleen said, then asked, "How's your hair?"

Olivia looked at her image in the mirror to see that Kathleen had gently flipped up the ends and scattered bangs across her forehead. "I'm surprised you could do anything with it. I've had to take so much medication for the past few months it looks more like a brush pile than hair."

Kathleen shook her head. "I don't know how you kept it looking so good living the way you did in Africa. I don't imagine there were that many beauty salons around."

Olivia feigned a blank look. "Beauty salon? What's that?"

Laughing, Kathleen thumped Olivia lightly on the head. "I'm glad to see you can still joke about things," she said.

Olivia's laughter faded to a wan smile. "I'm glad to see that *you* can still laugh."

"Yes. I guess things are never as bad as they seem," Kathleen admitted, then leveled her gaze on Olivia's image. "Speaking of things. Have you and Sam gotten any closer to putting things back together?"

Sighing, Olivia reached for the earrings Kathleen had purchased for her at the shopping mall. "Last night after you and Ella went to bed Sam found me in the den. We—uh—ended up having a long talk."

"Well," Kathleen asked eagerly, "what happened?"

Olivia fastened the amber drops to her earlobes while her mind replayed the moments she'd spent in Sam's arms. She could no longer deny to herself how alive he'd made her feel. "I told him that I wasn't going back to Africa."

"You're not?"

Olivia gave her friend a rueful little smile. "No."

Kathleen's reaction was a big sigh of relief. "Thank God. You don't know how happy that makes me. But when did you decide this?"

"It's not something I just decided. When I left Ethiopia I knew I wouldn't be going back."

With a stunned expression, Kathleen sank down on the edge of the bed. "But you've been implying that you were going back." Her head suddenly jerked up and she stared anxiously at Olivia. "You were lying to me about your health, weren't you? This strain of fever you've had is much worse than you let on."

Olivia quickly shook her head. "No, no. It's not that. I told you I'm recuperating. Don't I look fit enough?" She held her arms out at her sides as an invitation for Kathleen's inspection.

After studying her critically, Kathleen said, "I suppose you look healthy enough. So why aren't you going back? Why keep it a secret?"

"Like I told your brother. It's not easy to go around telling people that you've failed."

"Failed! That's the most ridiculous thing I've ever heard. You—"

"Kathleen, I failed," Olivia interrupted fiercely. "I wasn't strong enough to deal with babies starving to death right before my very eyes. After four years of it, I feel—I just can't deal with the emotional strain anymore. I feel dead inside. I feel guilty."

Kathleen made a sound of disbelief at Olivia's last words. "That's crazy. You gave four years of your life to help others. How could you feel guilty about that?"

With a tight grimace on her face, Olivia reached for a small bottle of perfume. "Because I should have been able to help more. Give more."

Kathleen shook her head, then asked, "So what did Sam have to say about this?"

Olivia opened the perfume and dabbed it on the sides of her throat. "He . . . said he was glad I wasn't going back."

Kathleen was suddenly on her feet. "See? I told you! He's glad you're not going back because he loves you."

Olivia wasn't so sure about that. Sam hadn't talked about loving her, only about wanting her. "He didn't tell me that."

Kathleen let out a short laugh. "Sam doesn't tell much of anything to anybody. Especially about the way he feels." She studied the grim expression on Olivia's face in the mirror. "Olivia, do you love Sam?"

"I don't know," she murmured. Then she rose from the bench and faced Kathleen head-on. "No, that's not true. I do love Sam. I think I've always loved him. I think that's why I've never been able to be truly happy since I left this farm four years ago."

Kathleen's frustrated expression turned to one of gentle concern. "Does he know that?"

Olivia shook her head. "No. And I'm not even sure I could tell him. Or that it would make a difference if I did."

"Olivia—"

Olivia held up a hand to stop Kathleen's protest before it could begin. "Today is Thanksgiving. I want it to be a happy one for you, and me and your whole family. So please leave it alone."

Kathleen looked as if she wanted to argue. But after a moment a smile broke across her face and she linked her arm through Olivia's. As the two women walked to the door, she said, "You are the most stubborn person I know. Next to Sam, that is. But I love you anyway."

"Thank you," Olivia said.

"I didn't give you a compliment," Kathleen reminded her.

"I know. I'm thanking you for loving me."

Kathleen squeezed her arm as the two of them started down the staircase. "In that case, dear friend, you're very welcome."

Olivia and Kathleen were eating toast and drinking coffee when Sam came in from feeding the hogs. After hanging his coat and cap on the wall, he fetched himself a cup of coffee and joined them.

"Mom and Dad aren't eating this morning?" he asked as he eased his tall frame onto one of the wooden chairs.

"They've taken their coffee to the den while they wait for the parade to come on," Kathleen answered.

Olivia pushed a plate of toast toward him. "We're eating light this morning," she told him, determined to appear completely unaffected by his presence. But that determination simply evaporated when she met his dark gaze. As she looked into his face all she could think about was the way he'd kissed her last night, and how much she'd wanted him.

Sam's eyes remained on her face as he took the plate she was offering him. She looked incredibly beautiful this morning with her blond hair fluffed around her face, her lips the color of rich brandy. He'd tried all night to get her out of his thoughts. But it hadn't worked. He'd been awake to see the sun rise, and he wondered if he'd had the same impact on her. "I know toast is Gallagher tradition on Thanksgiving morning. But I'd really prefer a piece of pecan pie."

Kathleen shook her head. "That would be cheating, Sam Gallagher."

He glanced away from Olivia and over to his sister. "Look at all those pies," he said, motioning with his hand toward the row of baked goods. "We couldn't possibly eat all those in a week's time."

"Oh, you poor thing," Kathleen crooned to him. "I'll bet Nick is eating all the pecan pie he wants this morning, and you don't get any."

He bit into a piece of toast and washed it down with a sip of coffee. "I'm sure Nick's girlfriends have supplied him with plenty of pies."

Kathleen chuckled. "You're probably right about that. But let's not tell Mom. I think she'd rather believe her son is pining for a piece of her own special pie."

"Well, when Christmas comes Nick will be here and we'll all be together."

When Christmas comes, Olivia silently repeated. Where would she be? she wondered. Still in Little Rock? She supposed she would be, although she had no idea what she was going to do once the doctors pronounced her fit enough to work again.

There're missions and shelters right here in Fort Smith that are crying for someone like you. Olivia knew that Sam was probably right about that. Arkansas, like every other state, had its poor and needy. In fact, she'd heard not long ago about a state project being formed to help impoverished children. The program, designed to address their basic living needs plus educational needs, had sounded wonderful, but Olivia was foolish to think she could be a part of it or any other charity work. Why would they need someone like her? she thought dismally. She was burned-out, dispirited. How could she inspire any child to learn and achieve, when she couldn't even inspire herself to pick up her life and begin again?

Kathleen gave Olivia a long, pointed look. "If you'd promise to come back and spend Christmas with us, you could help me deal with my spoiled brother. And my other not-so-spoiled brother."

From over the rim of his coffee cup, Sam watched the faint smile on Olivia's face slowly fade away. He'd learned from his mother that Olivia was planning to return this evening to Little Rock. She and Kathleen had tried to persuade Olivia to stay but she had mentioned her parents coming home unexpectedly. Olivia was planning on leaving after dinner. And to think of her not ever coming back was like being jabbed in the heart with a sharp stick.

Keeping her eyes on the coffee cup in front of her, Olivia shook her head. "I can't promise you that. I'll more than likely be working by then. I've got to start earning a living sometime."

Sam looked at her curiously. Last night she'd told him she wasn't going back to Africa to work. But now she made it sound like she *had* to work. Just what was she going to do? he wondered. "I thought your parents had given you a hefty trust fund when you turned twenty-five."

Olivia was surprised that he remembered. She took a sip of coffee, but still couldn't bring herself to look at him.

"That's the way they'd planned it. But after I went against their wishes and left for Africa, they withdrew it."

"Oh, my Lord," Kathleen gasped with shock.

Olivia merely shrugged, as though the whole thing meant nothing to her. But that wasn't entirely true. It had hurt her deeply when her parents had tried to buy her over to their way of thinking. "It didn't matter to me that I lost the money. I didn't want it. I'd always thought of it as bribe money anyway."

Sam studied her face, wondering if her passive expression was the way she really felt about her parents' actions. As for the Wescotts, Sam had never met them. Nor did he want to.

The fact that they'd put such outrageous demands on Olivia sickened him. How could they have taken away something that would have made her future secure? Did they not care that she was alone? That she might need help? That she might become ill?

He reached for another piece of toast, but stopped his hand just short of the plate. She *has* been ill, Sam, he reminded himself. So who did she have to turn to? You? No. You were just like her parents—demanding her to do what *you* wanted, what *you* needed. And when she didn't, you turned your back on her.

"Lord, Olivia, you gave up so much when you went to Africa," Kathleen said after a moment of silence.

Something in her heart compelled Olivia to look across the table into Sam's face. "Yes, I gave up a lot," she murmured. Much more than anybody would ever know, she silently added.

"Are you three going to keep eating toast all morning?" Ella called over the swinging doors of the kitchen. "The parade is starting. Come on and watch it with us."

"What about dinner?" Kathleen asked.

Ella gave a reassuring wave of her hand. "Everything is baking and simmering that is supposed to be. Believe me, honey, we'll have it on the table at one o'clock sharp."

Kathleen got to her feet, then reached for her brother's hand and tugged him up from his chair. "Come on, Sam. Watch the parade with the rest of the family."

He shook his head and headed toward the peg where his coat and cap were hanging on the wall. "I've got work to do, honey."

"What? Sam, it's Thanksgiving! Farmers give thanks for their crops on this day. They're not out working."

"This one is. I've got the hydraulic lines on one of the tractors torn apart. I want to get it back together."

Kathleen stared at her brother's back, then looked over to Olivia. "Today? I guess that means you're planning on plowing this afternoon," she said to him.

"Maybe," he said, tugging the cap down on his head. He pulled on his coat, then reached for the doorknob. "I would like to get that north field over by the river disced before rain hits. And that might be as soon as tonight."

Olivia watched him go out the door with a pang of disappointment. He probably did have work to do, she told herself. But she couldn't help but wish he would spend this time with his family and ultimately with her. She would be leaving at the end of the day. She'd told Kathleen and her mother it was to see her parents, but her real reason was she couldn't be around the warmth of the family any longer. She had to go but she'd probably be deluding herself if she believed that mattered to Sam.

Inside the building, Sam went straight to the tractor he'd been repairing. Parts and an assortment of tools were strewn around the floor beside the huge piece of farming equipment. He began gathering the things together while cursing himself for being so foolish.

He'd been hoping that the things he'd said last night to Olivia had somehow made a difference. He'd been trying to tell her that he still cared, and a part of him had gone so far as to think that she might come to him this morning and tell him that she wanted to stay here in the Fort Smith area to work, and to be near him. Instead she'd announced she was going back to Little Rock. God, he was crazy, he told himself. She'd hurt him once badly. Why did he want to open himself up to that sort of pain again?

By twelve-forty-five the table in the dining room was set with gleaming china and loaded with an endless number of dishes: dressing and giblet gravy, candied sweet potatoes, cranberry sauce, corn on the cob, green beans, hot rolls, an array of fruit salads, tossed salad and relishes, and of course the centerpiece of the table, the turkey.

"I can't believe the last three days of cooking have finally come down to this," Kathleen said as she lit a row of candles on an oak buffet.

"Why didn't you put candles on the table, too?" Olivia asked, glancing over her shoulder at the loaded dining table.

Ella, who was filling the water glasses, answered with fond amusement, "Because S.T. doesn't want to catch himself afire while he's carving the turkey." She stepped back from the table and gave it a final inspection. "Well, girls," she said with a broad smile, "looks like everything is ready. Let's call the men and eat!"

After everyone was seated at the table, heads bowed while S.T. gave grace.

"Dear Lord, thank you for this family, for the crops we've harvested this year and for this bountiful meal before us. And thank you, Lord, for bringing Olivia to our home again. Amen."

Amens echoed around the table, except from Olivia, whose throat was too clogged with emotion for her to speak. Her eyes glittered with unshed tears as she raised her head. She *was* loved, she thought. Maybe not by Sam, but the rest of his family loved her. Surely that would be enough for her to survive on. It had to be.

Sam, who was seated beside Olivia, saw the faint mist of tears in her eyes, and felt an uncontrollable urge to reach over and take her hand. Until today, at this very moment, he'd never stopped to realize just how alone Olivia was in the world. And he hated the very thought.

She deserved a family and love. And he wanted to give her both of those things. But how could he give them to her if she wouldn't let him?

"Sam? Daddy is talking to you."

Kathleen's voice broke through his thoughts and he glanced down the table at his father. "Sorry. I was just doing a little extra praying on my own."

"So was I," Ella said. "I can't help but think about Nick."

S.T. gave his wife a stern but loving look. "Now, Ma, don't get all bleary-eyed and ruin that pretty face of yours. Nick will be coming home soon."

The older man cleared his throat, then took up the carving knife and handed it down the table to Sam. "This is your farm now, Sam. It's time you did the carving."

Sam started to argue that it was still his father's home, too, but he could see that S.T. didn't want an argument.

"I didn't know this job came with the farm or I would have been practicing," Sam said, standing to take the knife and fork from his father.

"It doesn't have to be pretty, Sam," Ella said teasingly. "We three women are here for that."

"I'll agree to that, wouldn't you, son?" S.T. asked.

Sam looked around the table, first at his mother, then his sister and finally at Olivia. She looked radiant today. The dress she was wearing touched her curves in all the right places, and made her tanned skin glow. Gold-and-russet-colored drops hung from her earlobes and shimmered against her neck each time she moved her head. He wondered if she'd taken pains to look beautiful just as a way to torture him.

Olivia's blue eyes connected with his, and suddenly his heart jerked with the knowledge of how much he really loved her. "Very pretty," he murmured in agreement.

"Gosh, Olivia, Sam is actually giving up a compliment. I'm afraid the roof is going to fall in," Kathleen joked.

Sam arched a brow at his sister. "Just for that I'm going to give you a wing."

Kathleen laughed and winked at Olivia. "How did you know that was my favorite part?"

After Sam had carved enough of the turkey for everyone, the side dishes began circling the huge table. Olivia had never seen so much rich food in her life. Even by taking small portions, she was stuffed when it came time for dessert.

"You have to have a piece of pumpkin pie," Kathleen insisted. "After all, you and Sam were the ones who went to the trouble of digging the pumpkin out of the cellar."

It had been one of the few times she and Sam had spent alone without sniping at one another, Olivia thought. Maybe next Thanksgiving she could look back on that time and remember how it had been to walk with Sam in the cold, the way his hand had closed protectively around hers as he'd led her down the steps, the concern on his face when he'd asked her about her health. Yes, she thought, those sweet moments were the ones she would remember.

"Let's eat dessert in the den," S.T. suggested, scraping back his chair. "The football game is coming on."

"What game?" Ella wanted to know. "The Razorbacks aren't playing until Saturday."

"Well, our neighbors, the Sooners, are playing today," he told her. "And I don't want to miss the kickoff."

Ella looked pointedly at Kathleen and Olivia, who were at the buffet, dishing up pie and pouring coffee. "You heard the old man, girls. I guess we'll finish this dinner in the den. What would Thanksgiving be without football?" she grumbled, albeit good-naturedly.

Moments later, Olivia was the only one left alone in the dining room. At least she thought she was until she turned to see Sam standing at her elbow.

"Oh, I thought you'd gone with the others."

"No. I'm still waiting for dessert."

Why did it make her breathless just to stand in the same room with him, she wondered crazily. It wasn't fair. Especially when he appeared so cool and calm compared to her rioting senses.

Her smile was nervous as she looked up at him. "What kind do you want?"

"Pumpkin. Like Kathleen said, you and I went after it. I need to see if we made a good choice."

"If I remember right, you picked it out," Olivia told him.

"I guess I did," he conceded, watching her small hands work at placing the slice of pie on a dessert plate. "You can put a piece of pecan on there, too, if you want to, and maybe a tiny sliver of mincemeat."

She looked up and he suddenly grinned at her. It was an impish sort of grin, one that tugged at her heart. "I might—want to," she added coyly, then turned her attention back to the row of desserts on the buffet.

"Kathleen was right about those earrings. You look beautiful in them, and the dress."

The compliment was so unexpected that her hands momentarily froze above the pecan pie. "Thank you. Since I've been out of touch with fashion for so long, I'm not really sure how to dress.''

Sam wanted to tell her she would look beautiful in anything. Especially in his arms. But the words just wouldn't come. She'd rejected him in the past. There was no reason to think she wouldn't reject him now. And Sam couldn't bear it a second time. Still, he had this overwhelming need to touch her. To be close to her. To fill her senses and his memory with her image. Because he knew that all too soon she would be gone.

''Dinner was nice,'' he said, jamming his hands into the front pockets of his jeans.

''Yes, very nice,'' she agreed. ''Do you want whipped cream?''

''What? Oh, yeah. And don't be stingy.''

A faint smile touched her lips as she piled whipped cream onto the pie. ''How's your hand?''

Sam pulled both hands out of his pockets and gently flexed the bandaged one. ''Better.''

''If you'll remind me later, I'll change the bandage for you.''

''I will,'' he told her, then took the plate she offered him. ''Thanks.''

The soft light in his brown eyes shook her. More than desire, it was as if a part of him actually cared about her. Is that what he'd been trying to tell her last night? Either way, she was afraid to think about it. She was almost afraid to know. She wasn't ready to love or be loved, was she?

But that couldn't be right, Olivia firmly told herself. She was only asking for more heartache to even think such a thing.

''You're welcome,'' she said, then quickly reached for her own plate. ''Shall we go join the others? I haven't seen a football game in years.''

Sam didn't want to watch football. He felt more like going outside and cursing at the top of his lungs. He felt like kicking gravel, or a tire, or if he could, himself. He'd made a mess of things four years ago, a mess that had cost him dearly. He couldn't let that happen this time.

For the next hour and a half everyone lounged lazily in front of the television while the Oklahoma Sooners battled the Nebraska Cornhuskers. However, the moment halftime came, Ella got to her feet and stretched.

"Girls, we've got a dirty kitchen waiting on us."

"Girls?" Kathleen repeated, looking pointedly toward her brother.

He smiled and held up his bandaged hand. "Sorry, sis."

"Just wait till Christmas," she warned.

He grinned at his sister's threat, but his eyes were serious as he watched Olivia rise from her place on the couch. He wanted to ask her where she would be at Christmas. He wanted to tell her that he'd like for her to be here with him. Dear God, he thought, what was happening to him? He'd lived without Olivia for four years. Knowing she was leaving tonight shouldn't be affecting him this way. He could live without her again, he told himself. Hell, he'd done it for four years. That was proof he didn't have to have a woman in his life to survive.

No, he didn't necessarily need a woman to survive, he thought. He could go on working this farm. In fact, he had all sorts of plans to make the farm even better than it was now. But that didn't mean he would be happy. Not without Olivia in his life.

The dirty dishes were almost finished when Fred and Lillian arrived. Ella left the kitchen to visit with her longtime friends, while Kathleen and Olivia finished the last of the cleaning up.

"Well, that's that," Kathleen announced as she dried her hands on a dish towel. "What now? Want to eat again?"

Olivia groaned aloud at the thought. "I don't believe I'll be able to eat for the next two days. I think I'll go up and pack some of my things."

"Pack? Oh, Olivia. Why are you thinking about that now?"

"I've got to think about it sometime," she said, knowing as she said it that she needed to leave before dark and get the whole thing over with. But she couldn't deny that a sadness was stealing over her at the thought of leaving this family behind. And leaving Sam was something she didn't even want to think about. "So please don't start arguing and make it worse."

"Oh, all right. I won't argue. I'll go up and help you. On one condition," Kathleen added as the two women headed for the stairway.

"What's that?"

"That if you're still in Little Rock at Christmas you'll invite me to come see you."

Olivia slung her arm around Kathleen's waist. "You'll be the first guest on my list."

Sam shifted in the armchair and tried again to focus his attention on the football game. It was the final quarter and it would take only a touchdown to tie the scores. He couldn't remember when he had last allowed himself even an hour's leisure time. He should have been enjoying the game, but he wasn't. He couldn't stop thinking about Olivia.

Ella's laughter rang out, and Sam looked over to the other side of the room, where his parents and Fred and Lillian had a card game going. It appeared as if the women were winning at the moment. At least they were the ones wearing smug grins.

Restlessly, he looked back at the television set. The game had broken for a commercial and the local station was using the time for a short news brief. The reporter was urging everyone to drive carefully this holiday, especially since a cold front with freezing drizzle was expected to move into the area tonight.

Maybe it would arrive earlier than expected and freeze everything over. Then Olivia would be forced to stay a few more days. But what the hell would that do? a voice growled back at him. It would only put off the inevitable. She didn't want to stay here.

Suddenly his thoughts were interrupted by another voice on TV. This time a woman reporter was standing in front of a large group of people who were eating Thanksgiving dinner at one of the missions in Fort Smith.

"As you can see," the reporter went on, "without the help of volunteers and mission workers, these people and their children wouldn't have been able to enjoy Thanksgiving dinner today."

Sam pushed himself to the edge of his seat as the reporter continued. She was saying everything that Sam had been trying to say to Olivia last night, except for one thing. He hadn't told her just how much *he* needed her.

"There is a need . . ."

Sam didn't hear any more of the report. He left the room with a quick, purposeful stride. Out in the breezeway he saw Kathleen coming down the staircase.

"Where's Olivia?"

His sister arched a curious brow at his anxiously spoken question. "After we finished her packing, she went for a walk. I don't think she's come back yet."

"She's already packed?"

Kathleen nodded. "Yes. What are you going to do about it?"

His mouth suddenly went dry with fear. What was he going to do about it? If he told her how much he wanted her, that he loved her more than anything in the world, would she even care?

"I don't know that I can do anything about it," he said, then looked at her skeptically. "Why do you even think I could? She doesn't want to—"

When he suddenly broke off, Kathleen rolled her eyes in disbelief. "Sam, you're a hell of a farmer, but you don't know anything about women. Olivia is lost right now."

Sam grimaced. "Because of that damn job in Africa!"

"Don't you understand, Sam? That job was Olivia's whole life. She has no real home or family. All she had were those people she tried to help. And now that she's lost even them she feels empty." Kathleen paused as she reached out and touched his forearm. "She needs you desperately, Sam."

He stared at his sister as all she'd just said poured through him. "I don't know about that. But I know I need her."

Kathleen gave him a little push toward the kitchen. "Then you'd better go find her and let her know it!"

That was going to be much easier said than done, Sam thought, as he went out the back door. His sister was right. He knew all about putting a crop in the ground, how to make it grow and how to harvest it. But he didn't know about women. He didn't know what made them soft and vulnerable one moment, then all fiery and hot the next. He didn't know what they wanted to hear from a man, what they wanted most of all from a man. He'd thought he'd known when he'd asked Olivia to marry him. He'd been all wrong. Maybe he was going to be all wrong again.

Chapter Eleven

Olivia was walking down by the river when she spotted Sam's pickup heading across the fields in her direction. Was he coming out to see her? Just the idea made her heart begin to thud heavily against her ribs.

It took only a moment or two for the truck to reach her. She stood to one side of the packed ruts that served as a road between the fields and waited for him to come to a stop.

"Is something wrong at the house?" she asked as he climbed from the cab.

He shut the door, then turned to face her. "No."

"Oh." She didn't know what else to say so she waited for him to go on.

Sam stepped closer until she was only an arm's length away from him. He noticed she had changed her dress for a pair of black body-hugging slacks and a pumpkin-colored sweater. But it was her face that held his eyes captive, and as he looked at her, he realized how really beautiful she was, how soft, how vulnerable. He needed her and she needed him. He had to make her see that.

"You shouldn't be out here without a coat," he said.

Olivia doubted he'd gone to the trouble of driving down here just to tell her she needed a coat, but she wasn't going to say so. "I think I'm finally getting used to the cooler temperature. I'm not feeling a bit cold."

Especially now that he was here, she thought, standing only inches away from her. The breeze was ruffling his black hair and carrying the faint spicy scent of his cologne to her. It was a scent that was uniquely his, and as she breathed it in all she could think about was the way it felt to have him kissing her, holding her, and that in the days ahead she would never experience that sweet rush of pleasure those things had given her.

"I—there's some place I'd like for you to go with me."

He couldn't have surprised her more. "Are you serious?"

Sam cursed softly, then pushed a hand through his hair. "Yes, I'm serious. There's something I want you to see. It's important."

There was a look on his face, an edgy sound to his voice that made her sense he was spoiling for some sort of showdown with her. She glanced at him warily, knowing she couldn't bear to ride out another emotional storm with him. "Sam, I don't think—"

Before she could say more, he reached for her hand. "Just trust me, Olivia. Come with me, and then you can say what you think you have to say."

Why not? she asked herself. She'd be gone in a few hours anyway. What could he possibly do or say that would make her feel any worse than she already did?

Her hands lifted and fell in a gesture of acquiescence. "All right," she said with a sigh. "Just so we're not gone long. I'd like to leave for Little Rock before it gets dark."

"Don't worry," he said, taking her arm and leading her over to the truck.

Olivia couldn't hide her nervousness as Sam drove back across the wide fields and continued on past the house, then onto the country road. Where was he taking her? she wondered, and why? She crossed her legs, glanced at him, then back out the windshield.

"It looks like clouds are moving in," she said, feeling a desperate need to break the tense silence.

"Yes. The weather forecast is predicting a nasty front moving in. We might have freezing drizzle before the night is over."

Just what she needed, she thought, a feasible reason to stay on the Gallagher farm. But why was she wanting to stay? she asked herself. *You know why, Olivia. Because you don't want to tell Sam goodbye.*

"I hope not," she said. "I would hate to think of driving back to Little Rock on slick highways."

His eyes still on the road, he said, "I wouldn't let you drive back to Little Rock on slick highways. You should know that."

She looked down at her hands. She'd clenched her fingers into a tight little steeple without even being aware of what she was doing. She tried to laugh but the sound came out short and strained. "Let's face it, Sam. You haven't exactly enjoyed my being here on the farm."

He grimaced because he knew she was at least partially right. Her being on the farm had been bittersweet for him. "That doesn't mean I want you to risk your neck on icy roads," he said a little gruffly.

Olivia drew in a long breath, then let it out. "No. I know you wouldn't," she said softly, then looked at the rural landscape passing by. "But maybe it will hold off until tomorrow night, at least."

Sam looked at her and his heart grew heavy in his chest. "Do you really want to leave that badly? I thought you liked my home."

The question had her head swinging around to him. "I do like your home, Sam. But that's just it. It's *your* home and I wouldn't want to wear out my welcome."

Dear God, how could she talk about leaving so casually when the very idea of it was tearing him to shreds? "You're talking crazy now," he said, his voice growing rough with frustration.

Sam was suddenly impatient. And angry at himself because he'd allowed things to go so awry these past few days. As soon as he'd realized he still loved Olivia, he should have told her straight out. But he'd been so afraid of her rejection. Damn it all, he still was. He'd opened himself up to this woman once before and she'd left him wounded to his very soul. However, spending these past few days with Olivia had made him come to the conclusion that love was stronger than fear.

Olivia glanced across the seat at his strong profile. She was weary, she realized, so weary of trying to keep her feelings for him stashed away in a closed-off part of her heart. "Am I?" she asked, then sighed. "Oh Sam, the best thing I can do for both of us is to say goodbye. It was a mistake for me to ever come back."

Suddenly the brakes came on so hard that Olivia would have been flung into the dashboard if her hand hadn't instinctively shot out to stop her forward motion.

As the pickup rolled to a jarring halt along the dirt road, Olivia glared at him, her chest heaving. "Have you gone mad?"

His answer was to reach for her. "Yes," he growled at her. "Maybe. A little crazy. A lot crazy."

He didn't say more. But it didn't matter. Olivia wouldn't have heard it. She was too caught up in the feel of his hands drawing her into the circle of his arms, the strange, wondrous look that was in his eyes as he brought his lips down on hers.

By the time he lifted his head, she was breathless. Not only from the kiss, but also from the unexpectedness of it all. "Sam..." she began in shaky confusion.

"Does that show you how much I want you to leave?"

Her head moved back and forth against the curve of his arm. "I don't understand you, Sam."

His hand passed over her cheek, then tunneled into her blond hair. "I love you. I don't think I ever stopped loving you."

She closed her eyes. "There's nothing left of me to love, Sam."

"You're wrong, Olivia."

"I couldn't make you happy, Sam. How could I? I don't even know how to be happy anymore."

"But you'll learn how to be happy again. I'll teach you."

The feel of his arms around her, coupled with his softly spoken words were Olivia's undoing. The fragile threads that had been holding her together snapped, allowing the walls she'd built around herself to fall and expose the hurt, lonely woman she'd been for the past four years.

Tears poured from her eyes and streaked down her face. Her hands reached to cover them, but Sam captured her fingers with his and held them tightly against his chest. "Don't cry, Olivia," he said softly. "I won't be able to bear it if you cry."

Squeezing her eyes shut, she fought to get her emotions under control. After dragging in a long, shuddering breath, she opened her eyes and looked at him through glittery tears. "Sam, why are you telling me this, now? It—"

Before she could utter another word, he placed his finger against her lips. He didn't want to be told it was too late, or that it didn't matter to her. At least not until she'd heard him out completely.

"Don't say anything else. Please, Olivia. Not until we get to where we're going."

"And where are we going?" she asked, completely mystified by his behavior.

He eased her gently out of his arms and put the truck back into gear. "To a place filled with the true meaning of Thanksgiving."

Olivia could only sit in shocked silence as Sam drove them into the city of Fort Smith. She didn't know what to think, what to believe. He'd said he loved her. *He loved her!* Could it really be true?

The clouds were growing heavier, blotting out the late-afternoon sun as Sam drove through the city streets. Nearly all the shops and businesses were closed except for the occasional quick market and gas station. For the most part, the streets were deserted. However, when Sam turned along a residential area the scenery quickly changed. Here, children bundled in bright coats and gloves were out on their bicycles, or playing and wrestling in piles of autumn leaves scattered across the front lawns.

Sam made one more turn, then parked near a three-story house that looked to be as old or older than the Gallagher farmhouse. Cars were parked all around it, while some had been forced to park along the adjacent street.

Olivia read the sign hanging from a post at the front entrance, then turned a puzzled look on Sam. "This is some sort of shelter for the needy. Why did you bring me here?"

Reaching across the seat, he took hold of both her hands, then drew her close to him. "Why did I bring you here?" he repeated as he looked into her troubled blue eyes. "I brought you here because I've learned something, Olivia. About you. And about myself. All those years ago I was wrong in forcing you to choose between your work and marrying me. I guess my male ego wanted to believe that I was all you needed in your life. Now I can see how selfish and wrong that was of me. You couldn't be happy without your work any more than I could be happy without the farm."

Her eyes suddenly filled with sadness. "My work is over with. I don't even want to think about it."

"Don't say that, Olivia. Don't make me feel any guiltier than I already do."

Her brows drew together in a puzzled frown. "Guilty? Why should you feel guilty? You were the one who was right from the start. I was crazy to think *I*, pampered Olivia Wescott, could make a difference in Ethiopia."

"Olivia—you know that's not true."

She looked away from him as emotions threatened to clog her throat. "Oh, I know I went over there with a grand ideal and a stubbornness to see it through," she said with a shrug. "But in the end, I was just one little person in a sea of despair. It was like fighting against unbeatable odds until finally I grew too weary to fight anymore. Even before I came down with the fever, I'd become sick at heart, sick in my mind. I couldn't deal with the suffering and the dying."

The need to touch her, to reassure her made him reach for her hands and thread his fingers through hers. "It won't be like that here, Olivia. Sure, you'll probably see some pathetic sights. But you won't be faced with the extreme conditions of famine that you were trying to deal with there."

Her eyes searched his for the love and reassurance she so badly needed. "You're expecting a lot from me, Sam."

His fingers tightened on hers. "That's because I know that deep down you're a strong, giving woman."

Just hearing him say those words filled her with a bright, beautiful light. Deep within her hope began to flutter like the wings of a newborn bird, cautiously, but growing stronger as each moment passed. "I don't know, Sam. Right now I think I'd fall apart if I had to deal with one sick child.''

"I wouldn't ask you to."

"Then what *are* you asking me to do?'' she asked, still unsure of what he was leading up to.

The pressure of his hands drew her closer, until finally her face was only a breath away from his. "I want you to forget about going back to Little Rock. I want you to stay here—with me. I want you to marry me, Olivia.''

In her wildest dreams Sam might have said those very words, but Olivia had never expected to hear them in real life. Not again. It was difficult for her to believe she was hearing them now. "Do you really mean that, Sam?''

He lifted his hand to her face and brushed his fingers gently across her cheeks. "I've never meant anything more in my life," he said, then shook his head ruefully. "You talked about your mistakes, but I've made plenty, too, Olivia. I just couldn't admit it to myself until the other day when I walked into the kitchen and saw you there. Even with me biting your head off you wanted to help me.''

Her eyes dropped from his as she remembered how hurt and rejected he'd made her feel. "I thought you truly hated me then.''

He grimaced. "I hardly knew what I was doing or saying. You'd been gone for a long time. You obviously hadn't needed me in order to get on with your life. When a man's pride has been wounded it makes him act pretty crazy.''

"If you had read my letters, you would've known just how much I did need you in my life.''

Remorse twisted his features. "You can't imagine what it did to me when you told me about those letters. I spent half the night hating myself, and the other half wondering if there was any way we could salvage what we once had.''

Olivia could no longer convince her heart that she couldn't feel, that she couldn't dream or hope. She loved this man. It was all so pure and simple to her now.

Breathing his name, she flung her arms around his neck. "Oh, Sam, haven't you figured out by now that I love you? That I've always loved you?"

Groaning, he bent his head and began raining kisses across her cheeks, her nose, her eyes and finally her lips. Olivia was clinging to him by the time he buried his face in the curve of her neck.

"I didn't know. I was so afraid that everything you'd once felt for me had died during these past years."

She could feel a long breath shuddering out of him. And Olivia suddenly realized that Sam had been feeling the same doubts and fears and pains that she'd been feeling. Because he loved her. Dear God, he *loved* her!

Her hands began to shake as all sorts of new and exciting emotions rushed through her. "My love for you will never die, Sam," she whispered fervently.

Sam brought her trembling fingers to his lips. "Together we'll have a lot to give, Olivia. To each other. And to people like those in the shelter across the street. And I know that someday in the near future you'll be able to work again. I'll do everything I can to help you."

Together. The word echoed through her as she looked into his eyes. And what she saw there filled her empty heart. Yes, she thought, his love would help her begin again. Together they could give so much. Together they could do anything.

Olivia touched her lips to his in a soft, gentle kiss that took Sam's heart on a soaring ride to heaven.

"Does this mean you're going to marry me?" he asked, his voice husky with love.

A glorious smile tilted her lips as she tightened her fingers around his.

"What do you think?" she asked, then kissed him again to make sure he knew the answer.

It was well after dark when Sam and Olivia arrived back at the Gallagher farm. When they entered the house they found the whole family sitting at the kitchen table eating leftovers.

"Good Lord, where have you two been?" Ella asked with obvious relief. "I was about to send Jake and Leo out to find you."

Sam laughed. "You would have had to send them all the way to Fort Smith to find us."

"Fort Smith? What were you doing there?" Kathleen wanted to know, her eyes darting anxiously from Olivia to Sam.

"What were you doing?" Ella reiterated, before either Sam or Olivia could answer.

Sam's hand tightened on Olivia's waist and she looked up at him, love beaming all over her face.

"We were visiting," he said, his eyes never leaving Olivia's.

S.T. looked up from his supper plate. "I guess you and Olivia have a lot of mutual friends over in Fort Smith," he said with dry amusement.

Sam looked at his father and laughed again. It was a laugh full of happiness, because he knew that his father had already figured out that he was in love with Olivia.

"You could say that," Sam drawled. "We were visiting people who were having Thanksgiving dinner at one of the shelters for the homeless."

Kathleen and Ella exchanged surprised glances. S.T. wore a smug smile.

"A shelter? Olivia isn't ready for that, Sam," Kathleen said.

"You went to a shelter?" Ella asked.

Olivia's face began to glow as she looked at Sam's family, a family she would soon be a part of. "I thought I wasn't ready, Kathleen," she admitted, then glanced back up at Sam. "But your brother proved me wrong. Very wrong," she added softly.

"All right. What's going on here?" Kathleen asked in a sly voice.

Sam looked down at Olivia, his expression full of tenderness. "Should we tell them, or should we just let them wonder?"

Olivia smiled tremulously up at him as tears of happiness threatened to spill onto her cheeks. "I suppose we should tell them, or your nosy sister will badger us for the rest of the night."

"Tell us what? What *is* going on?" By now Ella was completely mystified, even though S.T. was sitting at the other end of the table with a calm, complacent expression on his face.

Sam chuckled, then looked around the room at his mother, his father, his sister. Soon Olivia would become a part of this family. A part of him. He didn't think he could ever feel as happy as he did at this moment.

"Olivia and I have become engaged," he told them.

"Are you serious?" Ella asked her son, then looked at Olivia and burst into happy tears.

"I hope you're all pleased," Olivia said a little uncertainly.

Suddenly chaos broke out as all three of them left their chairs to swarm toward Sam and Olivia. For the next few minutes there were kisses, hugs and joyous laughter all around.

"So when are you getting married?" S.T. asked when things had finally quieted down a bit.

"As soon as possible," Sam told his father. He glanced at Olivia, his expression hopeful. "The quickest date that Olivia will give me."

Everyone looked at her for an answer and Olivia began to stammer, making them all laugh. "I—I don't know—this has all happened so quickly. But—" She glanced up at Sam, her eyes conveying her private thoughts to him. "I've always thought a Christmas wedding would be nice."

"Oh, yes!" Kathleen cried happily. "We can decorate the house with white and red poinsettias. You are going to get married here in the farmhouse, aren't you?" She turned excitedly to Ella. "Mother, don't you think—"

Olivia began to laugh at her friend's excitement while Sam held up a hand.

"Whoa, now," he quickly interrupted. "I've got to talk to Nick about all this before you start making any plans."

"You have to have Nick's consent before you marry Olivia?" Kathleen asked with disbelief.

He shook his head at his sister. "I decided a long time ago that if and when I ever married, I wanted my brother to be my best man. So it has to be a time when Nick can be here." He glanced at Olivia. "Is that all right with you?"

Sam loved her. She'd marry him on Friday the thirteenth if it would make him happy. "Of course it's all right with me. I want all of your family to be here. And all your friends, too."

S.T. threw his arm around his son's shoulder. "Why don't you try calling him? I'm sure he'd be happy to hear the news, especially since he didn't get to make it home today for Thanksgiving."

With everyone encouraging him, Sam went to the telephone and dialed a number that would hopefully connect him with his brother. After being switched through several extensions, he finally heard his brother's voice on the other end of the line.

He quickly gave Nick the news while the rest of the family stood by listening and watching with eager excitement.

"Yes," Sam said, chuckling into the phone. "Olivia is that gorgeous blonde that used to come home with Kathleen. What? Oh—you didn't think I had it in me, eh? Well, there's a lot you don't know about your older brother. So will you be able to make it by Christmas Eve? I've told Olivia I won't marry her until you can be here to be my best man."

He glanced at Olivia and winked, then turned his attention back to Nick's voice. "You think you can? Great, Nick. Uh—if something changes, you will let me know? And that doesn't mean let me know two days after Christmas, either!" Nick must have said something amusing because Sam began to chuckle. "Okay. All right, I believe you. I'll see you then, brother. 'Bye. No, I'm not hanging up the phone, the rest of the family wants to speak with you. I'm giving it to Mom—she's doing a dance on her toes to get the receiver out of my hand."

Ella took the phone while Kathleen and S.T. stood waiting their turn to speak to Nick. Sam drew Olivia to the other side of the room to a private corner.

"Nick promises he'll be here by Christmas Eve even if he has to bribe his commanding officer with whiskey and cigars and drive an armored tank across Oklahoma," Sam told her as he drew her into his arms. "Nick hasn't always been dependable, but I'm taking his word for it this time that he'll be here."

Olivia smiled encouragingly, then slid her arms around his waist to pull him close against her. "I'm sure your brother will be here. Especially if he knows how important this is to you."

"Important?" he echoed, then chuckled softly as he brought his forehead down to hers. "I've never felt like this in my life, Olivia. Knowing you're going to be my wife, it . . . makes everything so bright and wonderful. I wish everyone could feel like I do right now.''

Olivia clung to him fiercely, wondering how she could ever show him, tell him, just how much she really loved him. It would take a lifetime, she realized. ''I can't wait until Christmas . . .'' she whispered happily.

''. . . When you truly become my wife.'' He drew her tightly into the circle of his arms. ''It's going to be the best Christmas ever,'' he murmured against her cheek.

''The best Christmas ever,'' she echoed softly, then raised her lips for his kiss.

* * * * *

Silhouette SPECIAL EDITION

THE DONOVAN LEGACY
from Nora Roberts

Meet the Donovans—Morgana, Sebastian and Anastasia. Each one is unique. Each one is...special.

In September you will be *Captivated* by Morgana Donovan. In Special Edition #768, horror-film writer Nash Kirkland doesn't know what to do when he meets an actual witch!

Be *Entranced* in October by Sebastian Donovan in Special Edition #774. Private investigator Mary Ellen Sutherland doesn't believe in psychic phenomena. But she discovers Sebastian has strange powers...over her.

In November's Special Edition #780, you'll be *Charmed* by Anastasia Donovan, along with Boone Sawyer and his little girl. Anastasia was a healer, but for her it was Boone's touch that cast a spell.

Enjoy the magic of Nora Roberts. Don't miss *Captivated*, *Entranced* or *Charmed*. Only from Silhouette Special Edition....

Silhouette
ROMANCE™

HEARTLAND HOLIDAYS

Christmas bells turn into wedding bells for the Gallagher siblings in Stella Bagwell's *Heartland Holidays* trilogy.

THEIR FIRST THANKSGIVING (#903) in November
Olivia Westcott had once rejected Sam Gallagher's proposal—and in his stubborn pride, he'd refused to hear her reasons why. Now Olivia is back...and it is about time Sam Gallagher listened!

THE BEST CHRISTMAS EVER (#909) in December
Soldier Nick Gallagher had come home to be the best man at his brother's wedding—not to be a groom! But when he met single mother Allison Lee, he knew he'd found his bride.

NEW YEAR'S BABY (#915) in January
Kathleen Gallagher had given up on love and marriage until she came to the rescue of neighbor Ross Douglas...and the newborn baby he'd found on his doorstep!

Come celebrate the holidays with Silhouette Romance!

VOWS
A series celebrating marriage
by Sherryl Woods

To Love, Honor and Cherish—these were the words that three generations of Halloran men promised their women they'd live by. But these vows made in love are each challenged by the tests of time....

In October—Jason Halloran meets his match in *Love* #769;
In November—Kevin Halloran rediscovers love—with his wife—in *Honor* #775;
In December—Brandon Halloran rekindles an old flame in *Cherish* #781.

These three stirring tales are coming down the aisle toward you—only from Silhouette Special Edition!

Christmas Stories 1992

Experience the beauty of Yuletide romance with Silhouette Christmas Stories 1992—a collection of heartwarming stories by favorite Silhouette authors.

JONI'S MAGIC by Mary Lynn Baxter
HEARTS OF HOPE by Sondra Stanford
THE NIGHT SANTA CLAUS RETURNED by Marie Ferrarrella
BASKET OF LOVE by Jeanne Stephens

Also available this year are three popular early editions of Silhouette Christmas Stories—1986, 1987 and 1988. Look for these and you'll be well on your way to a complete collection of the best in holiday romance.

Plus, as an added bonus, you can receive a FREE keepsake Christmas ornament. Just collect four proofs of purchase from any November or December 1992 Harlequin or Silhouette series novels, or from any Harlequin or Silhouette Christmas collection, and receive a beautiful dated brass Christmas candle ornament.

Mail this certificate along with four (4) proof-of-purchase coupons, plus $1.50 postage and handling (check or money order—do not send cash), payable to Silhouette Books, to: **In the U.S.:** P.O. Box 9057, Buffalo, NY 14269-9057; **In Canada:** P.O. Box 622, Fort Erie, Ontario, L2A 5X3.

ONE PROOF OF PURCHASE	Name: _____
	_____
	Address: _____
	_____
	City: _____
	State/Province: _____
	Zip/Postal Code: _____
SX92POP	093 KAG